FRACTURE PATTERNS

GAIL HELGASON

COTEAU BOOKS

The author would like to thank the faculty and staff at the Banff Centre for the opportunity to work on this book without interruption at the May Writers' Studio in 1993. Thanks also to the Alberta Foundation for the Arts for financial support, and to Stephen Dodd, Dave Downing, Dave Margoshes, Mary Walters Riskin and Coteau Books. Special thanks to Reg Silvester for editing counsel and encouragement, and to Edna Alford whose skilful editing and belief in this book are deeply appreciated.

Edited by Edna Alford.
Cover painting by Dan Hudson, "Orion over Andromeda," oil on canvas. From the collection of Joan and John Scanlon.
Cover design by NEXT Communications.
Book design by Val Jakubowski.
Typeset by Ruth Linka.
Printed and bound in Canada.

Many of the stories in this collection have appeared in magazines: "Bluffing" in *blue buffalo*, "Valley of the Rocks" in *Culture Shock*, "Shooting Menhirs" in *Other Voices*, "Fracture Patterns" in *Grain*, "The East Face of Sorrow Peak" in *Grain*, "They Don't Make Lakefront Anymore" (in another version) in *Secrets from the Orange Couch*, "The Language of Aggression" in *Wascana Review*, "Going Through the Gooseneck" in *Other Voices*, and "Surge Channels" in *Grain*.

The publisher gratefully acknowledges the financial assistance of the Saskatchewan Arts Board, the Canada Council, the Department of Canadian Heritage, and the City of Regina Arts Commission.

Canadian Cataloguing in Publication Data

Helgason, Gail
Fracture patterns

(McCourt fiction series ; 11)
ISBN 1-55050-086-4

I. Title. II. Series.

PS8565.E443F7 1995 C813'.54 C95-920137-8
PR9199.3.H444F7 1995

COTEAU BOOKS
401 - 2206 Dewdney Avenue
Regina, SK Canada S4R 1H3

For J.D.

CONTENTS

Can two walk together, unless they be agreed?

– Amos

Bluffing

She reaches for her double-faced pile jacket in the hallway, opens the front door and runs down the sidewalk as fast as she dares. It's only three blocks to the Jasper hospital. Wind-driven rivers of ice have formed on the hospital steps and Gabriella almost loses her footing. She grips the railing. She wonders what her grade ten students would think if they could see her, clutching the rail, as if the slightest breeze could blow her down.

Inside the hospital, equilibrium returns. The tiled floor feels cold, even through her vibram soles. The hospital is modern and all on one level. The corridors are eggshell white, full of promise, Gabriella thinks. She would have preferred vomit green. Even the reassuring medicinal smell seems diluted. The scent reminds her of the homemade cleaning solution she prepared at Liam's insistence. She used the mixture for a week, until she noticed that it took twice as long to remove grime as the concentrate she bought at the janitorial supply store. Liam hadn't noticed that she'd stopped using it.

The nurse at the station nods to Gabriella. "It will just be a few minutes," she says. "Won't you have a seat?" She can't be more than twenty-two, thinks Gabriella, three years younger than she is. She sinks into the vinyl couch. Only three weeks since the accident, and it seems as if she's been waiting forever.

On that morning three weeks ago, a light frost had silvered the clubmoss along the trail. Ahead, the plum-coloured peaks of the Maligne Range cut razor-sharp silhouettes against the sky. Gabriella noticed how Liam's thick black hair was cut as fashionably as ever, unusual for a climber, although his face appeared lined and travel-worn.

Gabriella hadn't proposed the hike until the night before. She'd called it "one last outing before the snow comes." She didn't want to let on that it might mean anything much to her. At the lake, she planned to bring up the subject of the lease. The landlord said he'd have to know by October 31 if they would sign for a year. Housing was so tight in Jasper; he had at least three people who would take the house sight unseen. Would they sign the lease or not? He always speaks to her about these matters, not Liam.

The morning sky began to cream with cumulus clouds. Below, in the valley, the dark greens of white spruce and tarnished golds of the poplars wove an intricate montane tartan.

Liam stayed in the lead. At times Gabriella had to run, the way her students sometimes did to keep up with her on field trips to nearby bogs and meadows. But she didn't mind Liam's pace. She sensed a special energy to the day. They'd be able to firm things up at the lake, the way they never could in town, knocking elbows, rushing about. She couldn't take the uncertainty much longer, now that Liam was talking about going off again for the winter, and she couldn't afford to keep the house herself. She thought that signing a one-year lease demanded a certain courage, a certain faith that the earth will keep holding them up, a certain commitment. She planned to introduce the subject in this way, as a challenge.

"Should get the lake all to ourselves," Liam said.

His boots left the partial prints of an expensive trademark on the soft loamy trail. His jacket was new too. He spent most of his money on outdoor gear – the little he made guiding American and German tourists up easy climbs in the Rockies. Liam liked to joke that one day he would have his photo in glossy magazines for high-tech outdoor gear. Prestigious companies would seek his endorsement. He always laughed when he said this, but there was a steel edge to his voice. He really believed it. She thought he was getting a little long in the tooth for this kind of fantasy.

When they were halfway to the lake, they stopped for a short break on a fallen log. They heard a man's laughter from somewhere below. Liam turned to Gabriella, his eyes vigilant. She had seen that expression once before, when Clive, one of the other mountain guides in the town, asked Liam if the rumours were true. Had he almost lost his nerve on Mt. Robson last year, when he realized the American climber he was guiding couldn't set up a belay that gave Liam adequate protection? Liam told Clive to go to hell. But Liam was secretly jealous of Clive. Liam has never been asked to join a big expedition; Clive was invited to Mt. McKinley last year.

"I'll handle it," Liam whispered.

Two young men approached. They looked to be in their late teens or early twenties. They took big elastic steps, as if springs were attached to the soles of their boots. Grey jays emitted staccato cries into the spruce air.

"Planning on going up to the lake?" Liam asked.

"You bet," one of them replied.

"Might not be such a good idea," Liam said, his voice thick with sympathy. "We're turning back ourselves. Came across an elk carcass by the lake. Some grizzly had himself a dandy breakfast."

"Grizzly, eh?" said the hiker. "Sure it was a grizzly?"

"Can't mistake those long front claws," Liam said. "They usually come back to the kill, you know."

"Guess you're right. Doesn't sound like a great place to be."

The pair turned around on the trail; the spring was missing from their step. When they were out of sight, Liam and Gabriella continued on to the lake. The grey jays had stopped shrieking.

Gabriella hears footsteps in the hospital corridor and looks up from a *Canadian Living* magazine to see the young nurse coming out of Liam's room.

"He's sleeping but I'll wake him in a minute," she says. Gabriella thinks she catches a quizzical look on her face. The nurse seems to be weighing whether to say anything more, then shows her straight teeth in a smile. "He really wants you to be here today, doesn't he?"

Gabriella nods. She doesn't know what to say. The nurse leaves her and pads down the corridor. Gabriella draws her legs under her. Her feet still feel icy.

Tell us what happened, the strangers said, pressing in on her with their uniforms, badges, khaki jackets and pressed pants. All of them urged her to tell. "To aid in our understanding of how these attacks occur," said one warden, a safety specialist, with a smooth chin and a particularly insistent manner.

In the end, Gabriella felt she'd fooled them all. Oh, she'd answered all the questions, but that wasn't the same as telling the whole story. How could she, when it still wasn't clear?

Gabriella watches as a merlin alights on a bare branch outside the window. Odd that he'd get so close. Then she sees the streaky yellow plumage. Just a baby. He thinks the world is a nurturing place.

Where is that nurse?

Gabriella looks again at the merlin and remembers how she taught Liam to spot wildlife. He said he hadn't really taken much notice up till then, his eyes were always on the peaks. But he wanted to know more. This was after they'd moved in together, before he'd gone off to Leavenworth with Clive for two weeks' climbing that turned into six weeks.

She and Liam had been looking for wildlife up on the Pyramid Bench. Liam couldn't see anything. Gabriella said the problem was that he was trying to focus on a single object. Instead, he should try to soften his eyes and take in the entire horizon. Liam tried this. He wasn't always willing to learn from people who might know more than he did, but she hoped he'd recognize her authority here. After all, she was the biology teacher.

They crouched behind a stand of young spruce. In a few minutes they observed movement at the edge of the forest: a cow moose, holding her head high, ears up instead of out.

"Means she senses danger," Gabriella said. "She probably has a calf around here. Better freeze. The worst thing to do would be to run."

They both froze. Afterward, Liam said he'd learned a lot being out with her. It opened his eyes, he said.

At noon Gabriella and Liam reached the lake. She found a rock of flat limestone along the shore and they spread their foam pads to sit on. Liam dug into his pack and pulled out a small bottle of Remy Martin, French bread, a wedge of Camembert and chocolate-covered almonds.

She felt a small rush of pleasure. He never lost the ability to surprise her, sometimes through astonishing small deceits, sometimes through extravagant gestures. In a way he reminded her of the plants and animals she so loved teaching her students about: organized, coded, identifiable as a type, but ultimately unknowable. Gabriella decided not to mention the foil-wrapped egg sandwiches in her day pack; she wouldn't dream of spoiling his surprise.

"To celebrate," Liam said. He didn't say right away what they would be celebrating but Gabriella took this as an encouraging sign. She planned to mention the lease after lunch. She imagined winter nights with Liam hunkered over topographical maps at the yellow kitchen table. Only this time she saw him studying places they could explore together, high meadows and alpine lakes. She smiled up at him.

"Clive and I worked it out last week," Liam said. He shook his crop of black hair and his voice pranced. "If we pool our resources, live in his old van, we've got just enough to get by for three months over the winter. So we're gonna head down south."

The words hit Gabriella like small, sharp rocks.

"I've had enough of this limestone shit," Liam continued. "Three months of good technical rock – I'm talking Yosemite, maybe New Mexico – is gonna make all the difference for me."

Gabriella grabbed for her pack and pushed herself off the rock. She strode as fast as she could without running. She didn't care where. Once she looked back. Liam was following her. Let him hoof it a little, she thought. She willed herself to walk fast and stay angry because she didn't want to think about what might happen to her if she relented one more time. Maybe there would be nothing left of her except endurance, maybe all her other strengths would be sucked away. She'd seen it happen.

The sandy shore of the lake ended and Gabriella crashed through a thick stand of dwarf birch and rock willows. A twig snapped and cut into her cheek. She hauled herself through one last bush to the end of the lake, where the willows gave way to huckleberries.

The grizzly sow stood twenty paces ahead. The bear's hump and dished-in face were unmistakable. There was not a climbing tree within reach.

In that instant, every cell in Gabriella's body yearned to turn and flee. But some inner force held her, a force she'd never before sensed.

Gabriella dropped her eyes from the bear's stare and slumped her body forward. She noticed how scuffed her boots were. She knew that if she retreated too quickly, the bear could be on her like a cat on a wounded bumblebee. She tried moving one foot back. The bear stepped forward a foot or two. Gabriella froze. The bear stopped.

Behind her she heard rustling in the shrubbery, and then Liam's voice. "Jesus," he said.

"I don't dare move," Gabriella told Liam. It took all her willpower to stay where she was. "Try backing off slowly," she said. "Bluff him, remember?"

And now, as Gabriella sits on the hospital couch, the part that was missing comes back. How she waited to hear Liam take one or two cautious steps backward. How instead, after one long minute, she heard the rustle of footsteps through shrubbery. Liam wasn't just stepping back. He was running away as fast as he could.

Gabriella hit the ground as the bear lunged forward. She intertwined her fingers behind her neck, legs drawn up over her vitals. But even as her forehead pressed against the gravelly earth, she felt the powerful sweep of the bear hurtling past. It was giving full chase.

The nurse is back. She bends down to Gabriella.

"He'll be counting on your reaction," she says. "Are you sure you feel up to it?"

Gabriella nods, but as she is ushered into Liam's private room she realizes she is no longer so sure. He sits propped up in bed beside a table brimming with gladioli, carnations, cards from the climbing team. She thinks he looks a bit like pictures she has seen of mummified Egyptian princes. Bandages wind round his scalp, over his cheeks and forehead and chin. Only his blue eyes, nostrils and mouth are visible.

What was it the doctor had told her after they airlifted him to the hospital? "No damage to the vital organs, that's the main thing." Then he'd listed the injuries. Gabriella had to bite down on her fist to keep from screaming.

"Gabriella," Liam whispers. She goes to his side. Broad beams of light penetrate the room from the west window and hurt her eyes.

"I'm here," she says. She places her palm lightly over one of his bandaged hands.

"Christ, I'm glad." Liam stares at her unflinchingly. "I thought you'd be here before this."

"I've been here every day for the last three weeks," Gabriella says. "You've been sleeping most of the time. It's just hard for you to remember."

"You know I wasn't trying to run away up there," Liam says. "You know that?"

"Of course."

"I meant the bear to come after me instead of you," he says.

Gabriella's mouth feels dry. She looks at her outstretched fingers, the irregular roof her knuckles and joints form over Liam's bandaged hand. She wonders if she could move her hand if she tries. For a moment she hears Clive's accusing voice and the bear's low grunt.

The doctor sweeps into the room and the nurse announces that they are ready to begin. The nurse starts to snip at the facial bandage. Liam's

Six weeks later we were swimming together in a tropical botanical garden on a volcanic island. My impetuousness shocked my sister and my friends but you expected nothing less, barely registered the faintest surprise. I told myself my master's thesis was almost finished anyway; I just had to compile the footnotes and find a better title than *A Study of Effective Preservation Strategies for Western Canadian Heritage Buildings.*

"Lynn, you're stalling," my sister had accused me while I packed up in our apartment in Edmonton. "You're finding every excuse not to finish that thing, so you don't have to think about the rest of your life."

My sister was twenty-seven then, only one year older than I was, but for the brief period I write about she seemed ancient beyond belief, she with her half-share of an optical goods store and new interest in long-term strip bonds.

"Give me a break," I told her. I guess I was too afraid she was right to respond with anything more than a cliché.

Most mornings on the island I read in the shade, making crabbed, frantic notes on footnotes, while you were tied up with seminars, abstracts, presentations. You were in demand and demanding; I was weightless, buoyed up not by pride, for I understood too little of your profession then to completely appreciate the extent of your accomplishments, nor solely by love, a word spoken rarely between us, but by what I simply perceived as the prismatic momentum of your personality. It seemed to me that you could curve one image of yourself outward, projecting exactly what the viewer wanted to view, and at the same time hold quite different images mischievously in reserve, to beckon as needed for yourself or for others. This seemed to me a most useful, if not a wondrous, gift.

It must be said that you also needed to exert a certain disdain, boyishly, forgivably, no more than a certain way you had of rubbing your wrists against bamboo place mats on planked terrace restaurants, where dark green waves licked up only inches beneath, or by the way you would grasp both sides of my head during lovemaking, vice-like, so that your hands reminded me of the blinders attached to the bridles of work horses, preventing them from bolting at some anxious anticipation of danger.

So many June afternoons you seemed to be able to dash away from your meetings; much of the time my thesis stayed in a manila manuscript box. Little mention was made of the graduate work offered to me in an Australian city, or of other decisions yet to be made.

We snorkeled off Kaanapali Beach; you followed a sea turtle in the bay at closer range than most would have dared. Your imitation of his lumbering form made me laugh. In Lahaina, tiring of hotel bars with names like "Old Whalers Grogge Shoppe," and giant clam shells and other ponderous South Seas decor, you reintroduced me to shaved ice at a rundown stand near the darkened beach. Real fruit flavoured the cone, not the mushed, diluted concoctions I recalled from prairie circuses. I actually chose passion fruit. Pinned the ice between my teeth and my tongue. Squeezed out every sugary drop.

That morning at the Pacific Botanical Gardens, we sneaked in at seven o'clock, long before opening hours, and walked in sandaled feet reading the signs for each tree and shrub: gum tree, African tulip tree, jacaranda, poinciana, plumeria.

You slipped into the water ahead of me, your sinuous body eel-smooth, curving around waterlilies with blossoms as large as human hands. I dove in and started to remove my bathing suit, wanting nothing more than the sensation of satin water against my pores. You shook your head.

"I thought that was the whole point of sneaking in early," I said.

"No, no, they charge a ridiculous admission here," you said. "That was why."

"But there's no one here to see."

You frowned. "Some of the guys from the conference were talking about coming out here today."

"But surely not so early?"

"You never know," you said. "Besides, there could be a groundskeeper around."

The suit felt sticky and cloying against my skin, the water heavier. You swam ahead without a sound and snapped a hibiscus from its stem, the kind the Hawaiians call Kokio Keokeo, or white-white. That was before I remembered a sign I'd seen at the entrance, stating that the islands have the highest percentage of endangered species in the world. The hibiscus petals were surf creamy and smelled faintly of vanilla. They rotted sweetly all week in a tumbler in our hotel room.

Near the end, which I persisted in viewing as the beginning, we walked wordlessly in a bamboo forest near Hana. How the forest moaned, low-pitched and keening, when the wind blew. You, with your love of flutes, were entranced; I thought it the saddest sound I'd ever heard.

At an evening reception I attended at the beachfront hotel where your conference was held, one of your colleagues acknowledged that you were making a name for yourself in the field of restored concrete. "David

Wamsley," the man said, shaking his head. He winked: "Don't let him get away. Or at least before he does, patent what he knows about cathodic protection for concrete."

You cringed from this kind of acknowledgement, but in airport waiting lounges you made notes for the engineering text you planned to write. Your field never did mean much to me: I grasped only that you were fascinated by the same medium that had built the Parthenon and the Coliseum. In your wallet you kept a photo of the Ingall's Building in Cincinnati, the first reinforced concrete skyscraper.

You winced when I asked if you'd seen *The Towering Inferno.*

"Concrete is hard to crush but easy to pull apart," you would explain, your hands never still, always building a structure of some sort as a child might build a steeple. You talked of how low-voltage currents could be made to flow through steel reinforcing bars in concrete to strengthen the medium; how you dreamed of building entirely out of reinforced concrete.

My work you honoured in your own way, which is to say that you asked few questions but made it clear enough to your colleagues that I was suitably overeducated for a man of your ambition. "This is Lynn Pojar," you might say. "She's an architectural historian. Believes it's always better to preserve than to rebuild."

"I'm actually still finishing up my degree," I'd try to interject, but by that time you might have gone so far as to mention the recent article I'd just published, with your technical assistance, on repointing historic masonry.

I don't recall the conversation ever going much further, and I cared not a whit. You had started your quick ascension and were gathering the necessary accoutrements; I was circling, half hoping to be gathered in, half fearful. You needed my good sense and solemnity, about which you teased me; I needed your recklessness, which vaguely disturbed me. Neither of us wanted that time to end.

Two days before the conference adjourned, I proposed that we take a day to see the famous sunrise on top of the dormant volcano and then hike across the crater floor. As I said this, we were standing on the fourteenth floor balcony of our suite, looking out at the polished bay where sails hung limp as white tissue.

"Samuel Clemens said no one should die before seeing that sunrise," I said.

You looked at me blankly, your eyes like the hard, black sand on island beaches.

"Samuel Clemens," I repeated. "Mark Twain's *nom de plume.*"

"Of course," you said. "I should remember that. My mother was an English teacher."

You were in a celebratory mood, still in dress pants, a white Armani sweater. You'd just come in from a late meeting with two civil engineers, Ed and Jay Ritts, who were looking for the right project engineer for a large development on the coast.

"They read one of my technical papers and wanted to find out more," you said.

I'd glanced at that paper myself: it criticized supervising contractors for sometimes allowing too much water to be mixed into the concrete, making it easier to work with, but leaving cracks and pores that exposed it to chemical penetration.

"They've got the capital," you said. "They're offering a partnership."

You grabbed me by the waist, lifted me high and spun me around on that tiny balcony. The sky and the other balconies above dissolved into a blue-white kaleidoscope. The last time I'd felt dizzy was when I was fifteen, nearly half my life away.

This week, when your name, and the names of those partners appeared in the headlines, and everywhere ordinary people scrambled to find out details of the horror, I remembered the exact timbre of your voice when you said those words, and the way the scent of vanilla hung faintly in the air. And I grieved for you.

My friends were less nostalgic; they consider that I had a narrow escape.

We had to get up at three o'clock that Sunday morning to reach the summit of Mt. Haleakala by sunrise. As I rose in the black-knit darkness, I placed my hand on the bed sheets; they were damp from our lovemaking.

I offered to drive the long, winding road to the rim but you said you'd be fine. In no time we left behind the moist warm air of the coast, the string of glassy bays, white-gold beaches and fields of sugar cane and taro. Your hand, resting lightly on my shoulder, detected a slight shiver. Immediately you closed the power windows.

A necklace of headlights appeared in the distance, angling up the steep highway.

"Unbelievable there'd be so many," you said.

"No more than to be expected," I could have said, and would have, with most other men I knew. Those were men of academia mostly, careful, worried men who jogged with their minds on cardiovascular fitness rather than sharpening themselves for board meetings. Men like Paul, the earnest linguist I'd been seeing before I met you. He gave me a revised *Dictionary of Preservation Terms* for my birthday. What I wanted was to drift over the city in a balloon, drinking champagne.

But I think I already sensed how you wore a shield of pride around you, and how it was almost as necessary to you as oxygen. It seemed to me then that there was nothing particularly harmful in this and that, to some extent, it accounted for your vitality.

Halfway up the narrow road you fell asleep. I felt the car veer and reached for the steering wheel just as the vehicle began to scrape against thin-looking guard rails. Beyond was a black void.

"I can't believe I did that," you said.

"Would you like me to drive?" I asked again.

"I'm fine."

The rim of the volcano was still shrouded in darkness when we reached the summit parking lot, ten thousand feet above sea level. Hundreds of people perched on the many craggy rocks and boulders above the lot.

"Come on," you said, your breath visible in the chill air. "We can get higher."

I followed you steadily up the cold, slippery rocks. Once I slipped when I stepped on plate rock, slamming my kneecap into a boulder and tearing my corduroy pants.

You found an isolated enough area where we could scarcely hear the crowd. But the air was even colder that high up. Chill wind knifed through the tear in my pants.

And then the murkiness of the night began to vanish, the horizon transformed into dancing planes of light: purple, mauve, coral, salmon-pinks and then leaf-gold, angling, leaping above the jagged edges of the sleeping volcano, bringing into ash-grey relief the cinder slopes and canyonlike crater floor. The ice melted out of my core. I felt as if you and I were witnessing creation.

"Not bad," you said, in your appraising, civil-engineer way, as a flash of green and bronze beamed across the horizon, and dawn shattered the sky.

Yet when the sun was only three-quarters visible over the horizon, you reached for my gloved hand and pulled me up.

"We'd better get a move on," you said. "I'm supposed to meet the Ritts brothers at seven o'clock tonight." You'd arranged a dinner meeting to review the terms of your proposed partnership on the shopping mall development in Victoria.

"Let's just wait ten more minutes until the Information Centre is open," I said. "I'd like to pick up a map of the trail."

"We don't really need one."

The route we were to follow, called the Sliding Sands Trail, dipped below the crater's rim and threaded its way across the moonscape of the crater floor before looping up the mountain. As we stepped over the rim, the sky began to soften to shades of rose and peacock. The flanks of the crater emerged sharp-angled, the surfaces like bolts of velveteen transformed by the light into rust, maroon, dun and buttercup yellow.

"Those symmetrical cones look just like mounds of sand in a kid's sandbox," I said.

"Actually," you said, "judging by the distance, they'd have to be several hundred feet high."

The air smelled burnt. Cinder ash dusted my white runners and I had to open my mouth wider and wider to inhale enough oxygen. It was still surprisingly cool, but I could feel waves of half-forgotten heat from those days two hundred years before, when the volcano had spewed lava in fiery lashes all the way down to the coast.

At first the trail was easy enough to follow, cutting through a vast wasteland bordered by the rim of the volcano and dotted with towering cinder cones. By nine o'clock we'd stripped down to sweatshirts, by ten o'clock to T-shirt, halter top and shorts. I handed you a bottle of suntan lotion to rub on my back.

"Just gob it on," I said. You massaged every muscle, soothing my knotted neck and shoulders. Your palms created circles within circles of heat that seemed to burn right into my bones. All the time I was conscious of the cool iron ring on your right little finger, the builder's talisman. As I stood on that crater floor, bracing to stand upright against the pressure of your hands on my back, it suddenly became clear to me how far you intended that ring to take you.

Years later, quite by chance, I met a man at a restoration fundraiser who had grown up with you in a dingy coal mining city in central Alberta. "Only then he was David Brachetto," the man told my astounded ears.

He said your father came from Italy to work the mines. After he retired he worked as a gardener in the town to round out a paltry pension. You lived in a two-bedroom house with a backyard the size of a postage stamp, the man said. Your mother worked in the meat-packing plant.

The sky above the crater that day was a bright, cloudless blue, the sun high. I told you of a Hawaiian legend I'd read about.

"The demigod Maui snared the sun from the crater rim and made it promise to go more slowly across the sky, so it would give the crops more time to grow, fishermen more time to fish, and his mother's tapa cloth more time to dry," I recalled. "They say that now the sun is careful to travel slowly. The name of this mountain, Haleakala, actually means `House of the Sun.'"

"Nice story," you said. You smiled and rubbed your index finger against the sweaty nape of my neck.

Waves of heat seemed to form quivering, translucent blankets. The cinder cones ahead danced, half melting and disappearing into the blue sky.

"So that's what a mirage is," I said. The only mirages I'd ever seen were on blistering hot highways back on the prairies. I'd thought of mirages as ugly and deceptive; now I saw they could be beautiful as well.

When we reached the other side of the crater floor, the trail divided into three directions. One path appeared to lead down the mountain to surrounding taro fields, the other followed along the grassy east slopes, while the third seemed to switchback up the mountain to the place where we left the car, a rough but fast shortcut.

"This must be the way," you said. I tried to remember where the paths led. I'd just glanced briefly at the glassed-in map outside the Information Centre. You were right, I was sure, but then my eyes felt tired, aswirl from the sun and the shifting heat mirages. My feet hurt and my mouth was dry.

You looked at your watch. It would take too long to go back along the grassy slope, you said.

"We should take the shortcut," you said. We headed up along the narrow, overgrown trail. Thistles scratched my legs and a cut began to bleed along my calf.

"Will you suck it clean?" I asked jauntily.

You didn't answer. The pace of your footsteps quickened.

"I should get a horse!" I said.

You turned. "I'll buy you a racehorse one day."

Your route took us up the dry, grassy-covered south side of the rim. The clay was hard-packed, everywhere split by cracks that created jagged pinkish tiles the size of dinner plates. The vegetation – sedges and prickly shrubs mostly – had a bristly, bleached-out quality. We could hear the traffic from the road leading up to the summit, but we couldn't see it. The air smelled of cinder and sweat. I had the impression of being inside a giant oven, the door only slightly open.

We must have been about two-thirds of the way up to the summit when we encountered the high wire fence. It was strung horizontally across the slope, as far as we could see, with barbed wire on top. The sign in front of the fence said in large letters: "No Admission."

The fence enclosed an expansive rectangle of the same packed, cracked volcanic earth, interspersed with needle-tipped shrubs. Here and there, in sizes ranging from a baseball to an enormous beach ball, we observed plants composed of spiked swords of a silvery aluminum color.

"It looks like something you'd find at the bottom of a sea," I said. You nodded, but at the same time you were taking in the fence, comparing the size of the openings with our bodies, no doubt considering metal fatigue.

I couldn't take my eyes off those plants, which looked rather like agave or yucca. Some were abloom with reddish-brown flowers from a central shaft. I wondered what it would feel like to touch those sharp-looking sword points. Would they draw blood, I wondered?

"I think we can squeeze through here," you said, showing me a place where the wire was a bit loose. "This will save us a lot of time."

I agreed to follow. I think now that I wanted the sensation of those sword-like tips on my fingers.

We removed our day packs. You held open a square of wire with your arm and your foot and I slipped through. It was easy really, even though with your longer arms and legs you had to manipulate yourself through more carefully.

Inside the fence the silver plants were so dense we could barely walk without brushing against one. The points of the plants, steel-like, scratched my bare legs. You were in the lead. You barely looked at the plants, and something in your purposeful striding made me want to grab you and make you stop.

Instead, I paused before a particularly large specimen and touched one of its spears with my finger. It felt like the edge of a sharp paring knife.

That's when I saw the sign, partially obscured by a stand of thistles. "Silversword: The True Wonders of the Islands," the sign said. It explained that these plants grow nowhere else on earth. "Not long ago, the Silversword was nearly extinct, due to the ravages of goats and souvenir-collecting tourists," I read. "If it were to disappear from Haleakala, it would be extinct, beyond hope of ever being renewed."

The sign said silversword blossoms only once in a lifetime, after as long as twenty years, and then dies. Even stepping within a metre of a silversword can kill it. Respect the silversword sanctuaries, the sign appealed.

I shouted at you, for the first and only time. You stopped and walked back.

"We really shouldn't be here," I said. "We could be doing terrible damage."

You smiled, in your accommodating way. Your eyes told me you would do this for me, lightly, good-spiritedly, as one might please a child.

And then we heard the voices. We looked up and saw a dozen people at least, at the far side of the fence, waving and shouting. We were about one-third of the way across the silversword sanctuary.

"Get out of there," they were calling. "You'll harm the silversword."

As soon as you heard the voices, you pushed me. Not backwards, towards where we had started, but forwards through the sanctuary. The heel of your hand felt like a cold steel bar on my back.

"Just ignore them," you said. And then you kept walking across the sanctuary to the far fence, in an unhurried way.

I followed you on that hard-baked earth, trying not to brush against the silverswords but finding them impossible to avoid. Each step I took seemed like a small murder. I'd never been one to believe that plants had feelings, but I swear I could hear low moans in the still air, sighs of inexpressible pain.

But still I continued behind you, and still the voices called out. They were becoming more and more insistent. "There's a five-hundred-dollar fine for being in there," a man's voice yelled. His words hung in the heat of the midafternoon; I imagined them outlined in big block letters along the rim of the volcano, a gargantuan arrow pointing down from the sky at the two of us.

After ten minutes or so we reached the other side of the fence. It was well away from the road, screened from onlookers by other shrubbery. Once again we slipped under some loose steel mesh.

"We've got plenty of time," you said. "We could have a swim before my meeting."

I begged off a swim and instead walked alone on the beach. Your dinner meeting went well. You would soon be announcing the formation of a company that would specialize in the restoration of concrete structures across Western Canada.

"Millions could be made," you predicted, correctly, as it turned out. "You can name my first racehorse."

I packed my suitcase the next morning when you were at your seminars. By the end of the summer I was in Sydney, trying to summon more interest than I felt in explaining recent restoration methods for Canadian woodframe houses.

A few years later I came back to settle in that prairie city. This was after I'd turned my thesis into a book that is actually still used as a text. Your company had become well-established by then, with branch offices all over Western Canada and in the Pacific Northwest. The man I married is also an engineer, although not your kind; he deals with highways and traffic flows, and prefers fly-fishing to racehorses.

Last Saturday morning I unfolded the newspaper at breakfast and let my toast grow cool while I read the lead story.

"It's horrible," I said to my husband. "Imagine, a parkade on the roof of a department store in Victoria simply collapsing. And fourteen people killed. People who probably went out that day expecting nothing more than their week's groceries."

The first stories didn't name the general contractor, but I knew. A friend of my husband's, who had once worked for your company, merely confirmed my suspicions at an office party that night.

"David's brilliant, that's indisputable," he said. "But there were a few rumours. Someone I know – a pretty good engineer – left after he suspected Wamsley might be low-balling to get contracts. Said he was hiring junior engineers to work on complicated calculations and then not getting someone more experienced to double-check them."

Some concerns had been raised at the ethics committee of your professional association, the friend said, although nothing came of it.

"We all knew a parkade was going to collapse one of these days," the man said. "There's too much competition, too much low-balling, too many shortcuts. I even heard that the parkade sidewalk wasn't included in the calculations, to make the bid sound lower."

Today there was a small item in the newspaper about you, saying you had driven off a bank in the Fraser Canyon. There's some doubt as to whether your death was an accident or a suicide.

I remember the touch of your hands on my face, on my back, the hibiscus blossom I found between the pages of my thesis draft while unpacking in Sydney. So paper-thin were the petals that they split as I lifted them off the page.

Valley of the Rocks

January 1

Dear Mr. and Mrs. Ogloff:

I didn't know your son, but I saw him shortly before he disappeared. The circumstances of his death are to some extent known to me.

Here it is a new year, and I'm still obsessed with what happened last year. That's why I'm alone at my dining room table this evening, working my way through a second bottle of Beaujolais-Nouveau. Lately on my afternoon walks, I've started hearing noises – noises that sound like the crunch of bicycle wheels on gravel. These noises seem to be getting louder, and I cannot understand where they are coming from. It occurred to me a few minutes ago that if I just pour myself another glass of wine and tell you everything I know, I might be able to drive those sounds away.

I first saw your son around noon last September 12. As far as I can tell from the newspaper reports, he disappeared later that day. What a cold and drizzly day to be in the

Canadian Rockies, especially at that elevation. Sleet was falling at the gondola lifts where I started out.

In a way, I rejoiced in the cold. I thought I would have the trail to myself. The sleet let up by the time I reached Citadel Pass. The dark spruce on the mountain slopes, with golden larch here and there, could have made the cover of my favorite magazines, *Backpacking* and *National Geographic.* I'd been poring over them, thinking about the trip.

It was through my late husband, Galt, that I first experienced the wilderness. I mention Galt partly because I'm certain I miss him as much as you miss your son. We hiked to Egypt Lake one September, on our first backpacking trip together, and now I've vowed to hike in the same mountains each September. In a way, that annual trip is sacred to me.

I became aware of your son when I was halfway down Citadel Pass. A voice behind me shouted "Track" and I almost jumped out of my hiking boots. Your son whizzed by in a blur of Lycra and aluminum. He had his head bent down and he rode that mountain bike like a rodeo bronc. He sailed down parts of the trail so treacherous I had to just inch along them, gripping my walking stick, even though I'm only thirty-five and considered athletic.

And then your son disappeared into the mist.

To be absolutely frank, my first thought was that mountain bikes are not allowed on that trail. My second thought – more of a feeling, really – was that some of the magic had gone out of the day. The encounter reminded me of the time Galt and I found the perfect camp spot up in Yoho National Park, beside a stream. And just after we'd put up the tent, two RVs rolled in. Minutes later, five families and as many ghetto-blasters flanked our campsite.

I could tell right away that your son wasn't planning to stay overnight in the back country. He just had that little fanny pack. So he could be eating at some burger joint in Calgary the same night. Here I was on my way to a lodge with no electricity, and no road in, only a dirt trail, just the way things have been in these mountain valleys for sixty years. And then your son came barging along on his alloy horse and stole something away.

Please don't think I'm a crackpot about technology, though. Earlier tonight I heated dinner in a microwave and watched a documentary on Yosemite which I pretaped on the video cassette recorder. It's just that too much technology in the wilderness makes me feel there's nowhere to escape.

Galt felt even more strongly about this. That first time, up at Egypt Lake, he criticized me for taking along a Canon Sureshot. He said he didn't like to think of the wilderness being packaged into paper squares and rectangles.

I just said, "To hell with you, Galt, I'm carrying the damn camera, and taking as many pictures as I want," and he didn't try to stop me. He always said there was no stopping me once I'd made up my mind about something, which can be pretty fast.

So Galt didn't try to keep me from taking photographs, but he always refused to hold still for the camera. The last snapshot I have of him shows his face slightly out of focus, standing in the door of the ski chalet, peering up at the peaks, looking like a cross between a high school track star and a philosopher king.

Galt was far and away the best looking man in a mountain climbing course I took in Jasper ten years ago. I noticed him at once. He actually managed to look trim in baggy gray jogging pants. On the second day, we were divided into two groups for a practice climb. I was supposed to go with another group, but at the last moment I walked over to where Galt was standing, and tied on.

When we finished the course that afternoon, we exchanged cards. I remember being afraid that Galt was only looking for a climbing partner. But he called three days later and wanted to go to a movie. We went to see Clint Eastwood climbing the Eiger, and joked about how many celluloid bodies had tumbled down the mountain.

Galt died last winter, and the way he died will help me to explain what happened to your son. I've enclosed a Xeroxed clipping of the account that appeared in the paper:

> *Banff - Galt Hagan, 43, of Edmonton, died Tuesday of internal injuries sustained in a skiing accident Sunday at Lake Louise.*
>
> *RCMP said Hagan, the co-owner of a computer software company, was struck by another skier while halfway down an advanced run.*

The police told me the skier who hit my husband had been wearing one of those ski jackets that have a radio built into the collar. The volume was on high when the accident occurred.

"The guy said he was just skiing along in his own world, getting off on the music and the slopes," the policeman said. "He didn't see your husband until it was too late."

I mustn't write too much more about Galt, and my own sorrow, except to explain the connections with your son's death. As I said, a drizzle started up again just before I started through the Valley of the Rocks. In that dark and isolated valley, deep in the wilderness, huge angular boulders face the famous mountain. I can never help imagining the Valley of the Rocks as a place of terrible rites. When Galt and I first hiked through here, I told him I thought it was an alpine Stonehenge. I even wondered for a minute if the natives who considered the mountain sacred ever used this valley for human sacrifices. Galt pointed out that I was confusing it with the Waipio Valley in Hawaii, where we had once camped. Afterwards we discovered that hundreds of virgins had been ceremonially sacrificed on a large flat rock not far from our campsite. I felt uneasy when I learned about the virgins, as if I should somehow have been able to sense the secrets the valley held.

The way I usually deal with anxiety is to picture calm scenes. So on that day in September after I encountered your son, I imagined arriving at the log-hewn lodge. I thought about the sauna I'd have before dinner, and about whether I would feel like chatting with the other guests, who would likely be quite well-traveled, or if I just wanted to retreat, as I usually do, under a thick down quilt, and wake up fresh the next morning to hike up to Wonder Pass.

I was halfway through the Valley of Rocks when the drizzle let up and I heard the music. I don't know the name of the band, but I'm sure it was something like The Dead Toads. Then I saw your son. He was sitting on a rock about five metres off the trail, rewrapping a nasty-looking gash on his leg with a blood-soaked bandanna handkerchief. His shirt was streaked with mud. He had a small cassette player beside him. The volume was turned up high.

Your son looked as if he was sort of expecting me to say

something. I keep trying to picture his face now, and all I remember is the thick brown hair, surprisingly clean, and how thin he was. Later, I read in the paper that he'd just won a math scholarship.

If your son hadn't been playing the radio, I might have stopped and asked if he needed help. I had a first-aid kit with me. But I thought he would ask for assistance if he required it. Besides, I wasn't in the mood for conversation. So I just nodded and kept walking. I wanted to get to the lodge by dinner time.

Before long I saw the famous mountain ahead of me, the one the Indians called "Place of the Spirit." I started to pull out my trail guide, to find out how far I had left to hike, when I heard the sound of the radio again and realized that your son was not far behind. He caught up to me, and we spoke for just a few minutes. He was very polite. If only he had been rude, what happened would have been easier to bear.

"Excuse me, miss," he said. "I wanted to ask you back there – could you check something in the trail guide for me?"

I nodded.

"Could you tell me how far I am from the trailhead?" he asked. "I'll need to get back before the last gondola goes down at six."

I wondered why he hadn't brought a watch, or his own guidebook? But I just looked in the trail guide and told him he had twenty kilometres to go back, up a pass. It was 4:30 p.m.

"Jesus," he said. "Like, I am going to have to have wings to make it back."

Then he considered for a moment, and asked: "How far on to that lodge?"

I told him the truth. The lodge was about eight kilometres farther, hidden in a stand of spruce. "You'll probably just make it to the gondola lifts if you head back now," I said.

I remember that he looked up at the pewter sky.

"Yeah," he said. "Thanks."

I kept on walking down the trail. I had a slight headache and a soreness in my back.

A fine sleet started up again a few minutes later. By the time I reached the lodge, the snow enveloped me like a thick woollen wrap.

The lodge appeared unchanged since the last time Galt and I were there. In the dining hall, reflected candlelight still gleamed on the polished surface of the pine table; sepia photographs of skiing pioneers of the Canadian Rockies adorned the walls. I hung my wet jacket and mitts above the stone fireplace to dry, and ate dinner: avocado soup, lamb with dill, rice pilaf, salade nicoise, dry white wine, fresh peaches in Sauterne.

"And how was the hike in?" a doctor's wife from Portland asked me as she passed the pilaf. The glint of her gold and ruby rings flashed on the table top.

"Brisk," I replied.

"Anyone else on the trail?" asked the proprietor. You probably remember him being quoted in the newspaper reports. He's a certified guide, short and stocky, about sixty. He's dug a few guests out of avalanches in his time.

"No," I said. "I was the only one crazy enough to be out there – except for one mountain biker."

"And are you hiking out too?," the doctor's wife asked. She glanced out the front window where snowflakes swirled in the blackness. "Or are you going to be sensible like us, and take the helicopter?"

I peered into my wine glass. "I'm going to be sensible," I heard myself saying. I was the only one who seemed at all surprised.

Climbing into the helicopter two days later, I felt a childlike wonder. A panorama of new-born whiteness spread out below, and I could see all but the peak of the big mountain.

"Helluva storm," the pilot shouted over the whine of the machine. "Never seen anything like it so early."

From the heliport, I arranged to catch a ride down to my car with the pilot. We didn't talk much. The pilot's van rattled along the pockmarked road and his ash tray overflowed onto the tattered oxblood carpet.

In the resort town, I stopped at a self-serve, gassed up, then hurried inside to buy a sandwich for the drive back to

Edmonton. On the cashier's counter, I noticed the headline on the front page of the Calgary newspaper.

"Mountain Biker Missing in Storm," I read. *"Wardens said they would resume their search this morning for a mountain biker missing on a day trip into the Valley of the Rocks."*

The paper didn't give the biker's name. I wondered then if I should call someone, try to explain. But I could think of at least ten good reasons for keeping silent. I should have reported what I knew earlier, of course; there would have been questions about why I had delayed. There could be legal complications. And I thought there was still a chance your son would be found alive.

About a week later, Canadian Press reported that the body of a man identified as your son had been discovered near the horse camp north of the lodge. Under a subhead entitled *"Loves Back Country,"* the story quoted Mrs. Ogloff saying that her son loved his mountain bike because it allowed him to travel so far into the back country *"without having to take a tent and sleeping bag."*

I wondered if I should contact you then. But again I found reasons not to. Now, for my own reasons, I feel compelled to describe to you exactly what I know of your son's disappearance.

By five o'clock that September afternoon, the peaks disappeared again under rain clouds. I started to check my watch every fifteen minutes or so, trying to figure out how much farther I had to go.

The light was faint by the time I got to the last fork in the trail, near the end of the Valley of the Rocks. A weather-beaten sign on a pole pointed south, to the lodge. And just at that point, I thought I heard the radio a long way off, but getting closer. Sound travels so far in the mountains.

And all of a sudden I could hear that radio in the rinds of my nerves, appearing along the trail to Wonder Pass, or on the deck at the lodge, just as the guests enjoyed an aperitif after a day's hiking. I envisaged your son hanging around, maybe playing his radio in his room, not really fitting in.

And before I really knew what I was doing, I was twisting the sign around. The sign was old, not the type the parks department has been placing in newer areas like Kananaskis, and a solid week of rain had made the earth sodden. When I finished twisting, the sign to the lodge actually pointed north to a horse camp about twenty kilometres away.

It was too cold to stand around. So I just walked on. I never saw your son again.

It would be trite to ask for forgiveness, or even understanding. I wrote earlier that the Valley of the Rocks reminded me of a site of human sacrifice. I realize that I shall always think of it as a place of dark forces and compulsions. Certainly I will never return.

Yours truly,
Alexandra Hagan

I place the letter in an envelope and address it with care. My handwriting has been deteriorating these last few pages, no doubt because I've polished off both bottles.

I walk into the kitchen, open the lid of the garbage container and tear the letter into little shreds. As I noted in the letter, nothing I could do now could bring that boy back, and even in the shape I'm in, I'm certainly aware that the letter could result in unpleasant legal implications.

I consider carting the bag out to the garbage container in the back lane before I go to bed, but change my mind. It's dark and late; there's no moon.

SHOOTING MENHIRS

I'LL WALK UP FROM THE VILLAGE, I tell my brother. It'll be better that way. Give me a chance to study the evening light. The narrow road inclines sharply. The thinning soles of my Brooks trainers are scant protection from the cobblestone path.

Whitewashed coastal cottages stand on either side of the path. Blood-red geraniums bloom in the window boxes. A wedding party is having going-away pictures taken on one sloping green lawn. The bride has a mouth like a crimson bowtie. The thought of photographing someone like that turns my stomach. I run my tongue over my lips and taste salt from the breeze blowing off the ocean. The grass shivers.

When I look down I see the curve of Camaret Bay, the little boxlike houses of the village and the ring of cliffs dropping down to the Atlantic. Beyond the last cottage, the verge gives way to daisies, poppies, nettles, honeysuckle, and hawthorne. Not one car has passed by in the half hour since I started up this cone-shaped hill; the concierge said there's a more direct road on the other side.

I use an old trick and look at my feet for several minutes as I climb. I believe in approaching subjects fresh. Later I will wonder whether anything would have been different, had I looked up instead of down? Would I have made out that soft grey shadow at the crest of the hill? Would I have retreated back to the hotel, instead of continuing on to this high and isolated place?

"Mind if I drive up later?" Andrew asked this evening, when I told him I wanted to walk up to the megaliths myself. He wore his "aw heck" grin, the one that fools people into taking him for being thirty instead of nearly forty. He was turning a china cup around and around. His hands weren't even shaking, although the tight way he grasped the handle reminded me of how he once flung his school chess trophy through his bedroom window. All because my father said he needed a haircut.

"You know the rules of the road," I said. I tried to keep the old irritation from welling up in my voice.

My dead father is paying for this trip to Brittany. What sentimental wishes could he possibly have harboured, I wonder? He left provision in his will for Andrew and I to travel here together, to the land his grandfather came from, even though we don't know any relatives and don't speak the language. Now it only seems fair to try to make the trip a success. I think Andrew feels this too, in his way. At night, in village cafes, he reads chess strategies and I read Colette; we're starting to prefer each other's silences to bare rooms.

Beyond the last cottage the outline of the megaliths stands out against the silver sky. I finger the canvas case at my side and remember with pleasure the way the Hasselblad responds to my touch, all cold precision, a third eye without the timidity of my other two. People think you photograph with your eyes but they're wrong. You have to use your imagination to capture an image, to exquisitely balance such elements as light, mist and shadow. Once you do that, the camera does the rest. Cy Sietzlaff at the gallery understands this, which is why he still takes chances on me.

When I left the cafe, Andrew waved at me by curling his fingers up and down, as though we were kids. He's started doing this lately and I find it oddly disturbing. He is always thinking. "Good portfolio hunting, Tannis," he called. I know I was supposed to smile. He thinks portfolio is too formal a word for what I'm up to.

It was on such an evening, fourteen years ago, that I saw my first menhir. I hurtled up a narrow twisting road on this peninsula, exhausted from finishing the course at the eastern polytechnical school and then flying to Europe and driving straight through from Amsterdam. I had a map, two thousand dollars worth of travellers' cheques, a new Nikon and an assignment from a national magazine.

The giants revealed themselves to me at the crest of the ragged hilltop.

Two of them, twice as tall as a man, smooth-sided, standing about forty paces apart in a summerfallowed field. One had an iron cross on the top, such as Sir Lancelot himself might have planted.

I got out of the van that long-ago evening, climbed over the fence and walked until I stood between the giants. And at that moment, I could actually feel their strength pouring into me. I envisaged shadows of Bronze Age men and women, pushing and heaving the great slabs into place; I felt that I stood at the antechamber to another universe. I saw the stones come to rest, tilted to precise angles to the sun and the moon, reaching for something beyond this last outpost, the place Saint-Pol Roux called the end of the world.

I have tried to explain to Andrew how I find something inexpressibly reassuring in this steady reaching out, but he just smiles limply and looks away.

On that night, years ago, I framed the soft sky and the speckled tone of the granite, and in my darkroom thousands of miles away I intensified the contrast just enough by burning in, vignetting, dodging. When I was finished the texture of that stone seemed to push right off the print.

I stayed in Europe for the whole summer. By the time I got back, Andrew had decided he wouldn't keep on at the university. He started helping Dad out with the store, and wanted me to help too. I said I had better things to do.

When I got home I showed the print to my father's friend, Cy Sietzlaff, who owns a gallery in Saskatoon.

"A dozen that good," he said, "And you've got your own show."

I slowly enter the circle of stones, the Lagatjar Lines. Each stone slab except one stands at least as tall as a man; most are the height of two. There are one hundred and forty-three stones in all, some arranged in lines, some in semicircles, astronomically coordinated with the sunset and the sunrise. Some are like swords pointing into the sky, others are more rounded, with moss spidering up their sides. Some gum wrappers and bits of pink toilet tissue are scattered in the grass.

The light should be just about perfect in a few minutes. I want to backlight the monuments, get a clear resolution of their time-pocked surfaces and the enormous shadows they cast. I want them suffused in lemony silver light, upthrust like the towers of Carthage in a Claude painting. I wonder for the thousandth time about the people who erected them, probably the race who preceded the Gauls more than four thousand years ago. The guidebooks say the menhirs were probably associated with the worship of the sun or the moon. It strikes me that in a way I worship the same thing with my camera: the source of light.

I brush my hair back from my face. The wind blows harder than ever. Even with a tripod, I'll have to shoot at one/one hundredth of a second and stop the lens down to get the depth of field I need.

And that's when I notice, through the lens, a movement behind one of the megaliths. I feel a second of fear as a figure lopes out from behind it. It's only Andrew. He must have driven up on the road on the other side of the hill. The wind was blowing so hard I never even heard him. He smiles, in a way that barely acknowledges my existence. That well of irritation rises again.

The afternoon conversation comes back: Andrew sitting in the passenger seat of the rental car, shoulders slumped, mouth pinched, me skittering about outside, trying to get some unconventional angles of a cathedral. Andrew tapping his fingers on the dashboard. I thought, not for the first time, how his good looks are spoiled by his air of adolescence.

"Let me drive," he said, for the tenth time on this trip.

"I can't," I said. "You know what the doctor says."

"Fuck the doctor," he said. He jumped out of the car and walked back to the hotel. One shoulder was hunched, the way it is when he's exceptionally angry and enjoying it.

Now Andrew is in front of me. He's dangling the car keys in his hand. For a moment the keys catch the silver gleam of the dying sun.

"Catch me if you can," he says. His voice pleasant but his eyes cold.

I stand watching as he goes steadily back to the car and gets into the driver's seat. My throat tightens. The agreement with the car rental company clearly stated that I would be the only driver. Andrew must have waited until I started to walk up this hill, then riffled in my purse for the keys, and used the other approach to drive up here.

But maybe it's time to let him go, at least for the moment. This light won't last.

I back away from the giants, to a spot where I think I can get the sombre, muted perspective I want. I place my bag down on the grass, take out the tripod, double-check my film. I visualize the way the light will illuminate the dark purples of the storm clouds, and the cow pastures that slope down to the village. I find it profoundly comforting that the images in my lense slanted to the sky long before the Pyramids were built.

And that's when I hear the car. It sounds as if it's going flat out, bumping over the rocks, accelerating towards me.

The Indian grave stood on my grandfather's farm, just a few miles outside the prairie town. I have often thought of that grave when I try to understand Andrew. I think especially of a boiling summer afternoon when I was twelve and my brother fourteen.

"You kids, go stretch your legs," my grandfather said as we tumbled out of the car. "Looks like we could be getting a storm later on."

I can still see Andrew running ahead in the barley field, charting a silvery-green line of destruction. We each carried a small Brownie camera, bought wholesale at my father's store. The cheap plastic strap felt hot on the back of my neck. I didn't want to run because I was afraid of damaging the camera.

My brother and I played together a lot back then. I relied on Andrew to lead me to all the secret places, the drawer where our grandmother kept a homemade recipe for contraceptive cream wedged between suitors' letters written forty years ago, the boarded-up shack where Grandfather stored his Scotch and a dusty collection of arrowheads, the widow's lakeside cabin where my father's car was sometimes seen during the day when he said he was at the store.

On that hot afternoon, Andrew and I found a peculiar slab on the other side of the field, by a creek. The slab was at least as long as a person and came up to our knees in height. The gray stone felt smooth as the porcelain in our bathtub; three short horizontal lines on one end looked as though they had been cut in long ago by a knife. Right away I was convinced that we had discovered an Indian grave.

Andrew, who even then desperately wanted to become an archaeologist, said he'd go back for a crowbar and see if we could dig up a skeleton. I said no, we should take pictures instead.

Andrew smiled. "Pictures?" he said. "Wouldn't you rather see a real skeleton?"

I shook my head. I told him that if he let me take pictures of the grave as it was, I would never tell anyone about the arrowheads I'd seen in the back of his closet, the ones that looked like Grandfather's.

At least twenty minutes must have gone by while I took those pictures. I used up a whole roll. My father promised he'd show me how to make prints myself, and for once he did what he promised. I still have those prints in a box somewhere in the condominium on the coast: the barley bending in the wind, a cow in the field, a black cloud bearing down. The rock had more character than most people, in my opinion.

After I finished taking the pictures, Andrew and I started back across the barley field to the farmhouse. An anvil-shaped cloud raced above us. We could hear frogs croaking from the slough way across the road.

I wanted, just once, to lead the way. "Catch me if you can," I yelled, forgetting about the camera, and sprinted across the field, up and over a slight rise, Andrew running after me.

Afterwards, everyone asked what a lightning strike looked like. All I could remember was the sensation of white light and then a roar like a hundred shotguns going off, and seeing Andrew slumped on the ground.

I started to run for help and then I stopped. Lightning still flashed and it began to hail, tiny hard chunks beating against the barley stalks. I plunged down in the field, pebbles digging into my abdomen. Even after the thunder ceased, I remained there, hugging the ground. Did I stay ten minutes? Twenty minutes? I never knew. After a while I got up and walked back to the house. I just didn't seem to have any more energy left for Andrew.

When I got to the house, my grandfather called an ambulance. The Westminster chimes rang out every quarter hour. I remember sitting in his farmhouse kitchen, noticing for the first time how the old linoleum, with its pink feathered pattern, curled at the edge of the baseboard. Astonishment ran through my nerve ends like electricity.

At eight o'clock my father called to say that Andrew would pull through. The Scottish doctor said he was "one lucky laddie." A thirteen-year-old girl up by Esk had been killed the summer before, struck by lightning while playing baseball on a Friday afternoon.

"It's not so rare as you think," the doctor said.

We didn't play together as much after that. Andrew told me he didn't want to be an unpaid babysitter anymore. Poking around under rocks was for infants, he said. He never did become an archaeologist. When I asked if I could have his arrowheads, he gathered them up, ran out with them to the garden, and threw them in all directions.

"Yours if you find them," he said, in a kindly voice. I wouldn't even give him the satisfaction of looking.

He began to get tremors, so he couldn't drive a car or even take a photograph that wasn't blurry. He'd be having dinner, or telling a joke, or playing chess by himself, and all of a sudden he'd start to shake and he wouldn't be able to stop. My father said it was something psychological but no one could really figure out what.

My parents took Andrew to see the neurologists at the University Hospital in Saskatoon, and came back speaking in low voices about minor brain damage and epilepsy-like symptoms. Andrew stayed away for a month for tests. But the tremors continued. Once I overheard my father saying that Andrew might have suffered a grand mal, and that intense light could trigger an attack. But when I asked Andrew about it, he just shrugged and asked what the hell did doctors know?

When Dad died last month, I found in his bottom bureau drawer the T-shirt Andrew was wearing that afternoon. It had a dime-size brown hole in the middle of the back.

Andrew's done okay for himself, though, despite the tremors and his recent divorce. He always could see opportunity, on or off the chessboard. He expanded Dad's store, found out about discount places in the East where he could order supplies cheap and offer lower costs than competitors. Then he hired local people to do what he couldn't, teachers usually, happy to make a few dollars on the side and not too concerned about getting top dollar. He lets them play with expensive equipment, even allows them to use the studio sometimes for their own projects.

Andrew has a staff of five working for him. When I was back for Dad's funeral, he had one of his employees drive me out to see a new store in another town. Andrew doesn't dare drive anymore, he's got so many warnings.

The car accelerates towards me. For a second a dazzling ray of light glints from the chrome on the bumper. I stand frozen until I see the lion insignia on the front grill of the Peugeot, then in the driver's seat Andrew's head, his hunched shoulders. For a second I imagine I see him wave, that silly baby wave.

That's when I start to run, leaving the camera in its tripod. I feel my runners dig into the hard-packed dirt. I dash uphill towards the giants, as if the sky is about to fall in, as if something wild and fearful has been let loose.

The car sounds as if it's inside my head. I imagine the lion insignia crushing its imprint into my flesh. And just at that moment, I reach the circle. I dash to the spot where two slabs stand together, one smaller, like a stepping stone. I spring on top of one, then the other. The pressure in my chest is unendurable.

The engine dies. I look down and see the Peugeot halted outside the circle. Andrew gently opens the door. He looks at me for a long minute. Then he turns and starts to walk toward the village. I fix in my mind the image of my brother moving steadily away from me, buoyant with something as dark and solid and everlasting as the stone beneath me.

Fracture Patterns

SOMEONE HAS WRITTEN "CLOSED" ON a strip of orange vinyl tape and draped it over the highway sign. Kurt turns off anyway; we're accustomed to ignoring signs in this lawyered land, signs that say things like: "No Salesmen, Peddlers and Whatnots," or "No Trespassing. Don't Even Ask. Just Keep Out." We bicycle along the straight gravel road, eyes on the late afternoon thunderheads moving from the west towards us over the bleached-brown plains. My face feels as if it's been rubbed with sandpaper.

The road descends into a narrow Montana valley, where I can easily imagine a stagecoach pushing over the sage-covered hills. I catch up to Kurt and recite the message, written on a board sign, that once greeted visitors:

Tu grass Hop Per digins
Three myle
Kepe the trale nex the bluffe

Kurt smiles but, as usual these days, his attention is on what's ahead: a creek running beyond a clump of cottonwoods, and on the facing hill a dozen or so unpainted wooden buildings that appear to be abandoned. "So this is it," he says, and points to the remains of the town once nicknamed Grasshopper Diggins. I scan Kurt's square flushed face for a trace of what he's thinking. He gives me the same thin smile he's worn since he heard about the opening at the Quebec mine.

Just before the creek we encounter a barbed wire fence with a chain wound around the gate. We don't talk about what we're going to do. It's a given. Lately, though, I've noticed that some of the givens are disappearing. Has Kurt noticed, I wonder? Or is his mind too full of tracer tests, alpha-blasts, fracture patterns, velocity converts, waveform frequencies?

The wire screeches as Kurt hoists himself over. Quickly we lift the bicycles over the top and set up camp by the creek, out of sight of the abandoned town. The picnic table is spotted off-white with bird shit. Scruffy grass grows over the parking stalls.

Kurt looks across the creek at the reddish earth and gravel tips the gold miners left. "Can't you just hear the gunshots from way back then?" he says. I feel a rush of gratitude at the way he's trying to make this trip work. Kurt has little interest in history, except our own.

I leave him snapping together the tent poles. At least for once he's not thumbing through *How to Do a Week's Work in 24 Hours* or *Thinking Strategically*. I can tell by the way he holds his mouth open, tongue curled on one side, that nothing else but the task exists for him right now. If only Kurt could relax like this more often, we might not be facing another upheaval.

The sign at the last village said "Forty-five Miles to Services." I think of this as I walk along the gravel road to the campground pump. My footsteps stir small plumes of dust. The house closest to the campground is the only freshly painted building in sight: white clapboard, with shutters and cranberry-pink trim. In the backyard, woollen sweaters hang on the line: cerise, plum-dark purple, butter yellow. For a moment, I'm envious of whoever might live here, with only the slow-moving creek and the cobalt blue sky and the ghosts for company. I even speculate on what I might do if I lived here on my own, with all the uninterrupted time in the world.

I like to think of myself as something of a gold miner, although I'd never say so to Kurt. I try to mine the English language, not at the part-time job at the foundation, writing press releases and reports, but in my poetry. Even now, Kurt becomes impatient when I keep him waiting, making notes, so I'm learning to steal moments like this. I promised my publisher I'd have the Timson poems ready by Christmas.

I place the water container down on the concrete pad beneath the pump, and see that a small chain has been wrapped around the handle and the stem. I find a sharp-edged rock, stretch a portion of the chain and fling the rock against it. The rock makes a tinny sound. Again I hurl the rock. One link twists open enough to release another link. In that moment, an inexplicable compulsion comes over me to get back to Kurt. I pump water into the plastic container as if my life depended on it.

After supper we walk up to the deserted main street. "Must be the caretaker," Kurt says, as we go by the painted house. The front yard is bounded by a brown rock fence and swirls of blue flax, evening primrose, sticky purple geraniums and tough little bachelor buttons. I would have expected ceramic gnomes.

I think of our first rock garden back in Alberta, five years ago, when we were just married. That was before the moves to Whitehorse and Houston and northern Ontario. Kurt always used to bring back small shiny pebbles from his surveys up north. We'd ring our wildflower beds with them. By the time we transferred back to Edmonton last year, we'd long given up on that idea. It was too ridiculous, hauling rocks around the country.

A gold-panning demonstration on the North Saskatchewan River brought us together. Kurt was there because he wanted to talk to the aging gold-panner about a rumoured sleeper mine in the Alberta Rockies. I'd already begun writing the Timson poems and knew I had to actually hold river-panned gold in my hand.

I remember how I bent over the clear river water, shaking the pan as the miner had shown me, hearing the pebbles clink. Then I saw the glint of quartzite in the pan. I picked it out and rubbed the creamy crystalline stone with my thumb, and the miner laughed and said I'd be a sucker for fool's gold. And then Kurt stepped towards me and said: "You're right, it's very beautiful."

After the demonstration, Kurt walked with me beside the river and taught me the names of the other stones: porphyry, copper ore, feldspar, magnetite. I knew I was learning another language, with its own stanzas and metres and unfathomable mysteries.

Kurt explained that his field was a specialized kind of mining engineering. He had to figure out how to retrieve precious metals too expensive to extract by traditional techniques. He worked for the federal government, he said, but he wanted to have his own consulting company soon. Now, five years later, he's still with the government. But he says the move to the Quebec mine would give him the experience and contacts he needs to branch out on his own.

On that first day, at a bend in the river, Kurt took a pan out of his backpack. Within minutes he had sifted out a tiny gold-coloured fleck from the water. He placed the fleck in his mouth, then spit it into his hand.

"Gold, all right," he said. "Pyrites feel gritty between your teeth. Gold feels smooth."

I took the fleck from his hand, placed it between my teeth and ran my tongue against it. The metal felt as satisfyingly smooth as enamel.

In front of the old drug store and assay office, Kurt and I try to imagine raw gold being analyzed in that fitful time so many years ago. I kick at the hard-packed dirt main street. "They say that when it rained back then, the streets weren't even jackassable," I tell Kurt. He gives me that distracted smile I find so infuriating.

Then he says he wants to have a closer look at some of the old sluicing equipment. Secretly I suspect that he's preparing for the interview in Quebec, or making notes for that fall symposium on reagents in mineral engineering in Cornwall, England.

At first Kurt's obsession with the future fascinated me. All I could think of on any single day was how to write a few lines of poetry that really worked. I'd lived in Edmonton all my life, and I felt dazzled by the way we'd plan trips to Alaska, to the Milford Track in New Zealand. But somehow the trips never came off. And now that I'm balking at the Quebec move, Kurt actually accuses me of caring more for the Timson poems than I do about him. I've stopped showing him the poems, or even talking about Rebecca Timson.

I leave Kurt gazing at the Methodist church, one of the oldest in the state, and the jails across the street. I know what I've come all the way from Alberta to see, and I want to have a good look before Kurt again becomes restless.

I hurry on to Skinner's saloon. The one-storey wooden building must have lost its paint even before the town was abandoned in 1938. I push the door and it grunts open. The black air inside smells like rotted earth. Gradually I make out the bare planked floor, the copper-topped bar along the west wall, the rat poison stacked at the back of the building.

Then I turn and see the barber chair in the other corner, and the shock of the barber's story comes back to me. I have read much about the barber who owned this building, who came to such a terrible end. What conversations of betrayal must have taken place around that chair? I wonder. What must Buck Timson have been like, to have cut his neighbors' hair and trimmed their mustaches during the day, and then do what he did at night? And I see in my mind Rebecca Timson, whose story I have so often tried to tell in my poems and failed, and I think I am starting to see why.

I turn towards the door and start.

"Sorry if I frightened you, love," a woman says. Her outline is framed by crepuscular light. I have the impression of someone willowy and fast-moving.

When my eyes readjust, I see a tall woman likely in her early forties, older than her quick movements have prepared me for. She has marmalade hair streaked with grey, carelessly touching her shoulders, and eyes the colour of cactus. She is wearing jeans, a wool sweater of the most exquisite leaf-green I have ever seen, matching socks and expensive leather loafers. Something about the woman – her offhandedness, the creaminess of her voice – makes me feel she's after something.

I look for Kurt but he's not in sight.

"Are you the caretaker?" I ask.

The woman nods. She tells me her name is Ollwyn Franklin.

"I didn't hear your vehicle," she says, warmly.

I explain that we're on bicycles, that we drove down from Alberta and left the car in Missoula to do some bike-touring for a week.

"The tourist information place in Missoula assured us the site would be open by June, so when we saw the sign we decided to come anyway. We don't need much, the way we camp."

The woman smiles. "The campground is closed, but since you came on bicycles I guess you can stay," she says. "It's getting late to be finding another place. I'm afraid there's no water. And I can't really spare any myself. My husband's supposed to bring another barrel when he comes back from Dillon, but that won't be for two days."

I lie and say that we brought enough for tonight. I don't want to admit that I've broken the chain on the pump. "Any chance of getting in to see the museum?" I ask.

The woman shrugs. "Ask me in the morning," she says. Some of the creaminess has gone out of her voice. Then she turns back and asks: "The gate is still locked, isn't it?"

I assure her that it is.

Kurt appears suddenly, making me laugh by saying that he's just gotten out of jail. I introduce him to Mrs. Franklin, and for a moment imagine I see him as a stranger might, a tall man in his mid-thirties, with sun-glazed skin, a limber, forceful athlete's body disguising the restlessness inside.

And I remember the words of my friend, Lorna: "You're complaining because he wants to take you to places like Cornwall and New Guinea and Arizona?" she said. "I should be so lucky."

I started to explain how I felt, but then I remembered that Lorna is an actress, at home on any stage. My own art requires peace and order. I like to go to my old desk and look out on the city where I grew up, and if I'm still enough, and quiet enough, I find the words I'm looking for.

Back at the campground, Kurt and I make hot chocolate from the water that sits in the container on top of the picnic table. It's blue from the water purification pills Kurt uses. He's like that, careful, attentive to details. I watch as he unfolds my sleeping bag, shaking it violently so the feathers will loft. Suddenly Kurt stops and looks at me. I'm afraid he's going to say that he wants to leave right away tomorrow morning, but he surprises me.

"I saw the way you looked at that garden," he says.

I nod. I didn't think I needed things like gardens when we got married, but then I didn't think we'd be moving three times in five years. Each time things will be better, Kurt says, but he's not the one who gets stuck changing a dozen magazine subscriptions. When we moved back from the north last year, the moving company lost a crate of books that contained a rare edition of early pioneer poetry by Western Canadian women, the one that moved me to write my first poem.

Lately Kurt has been surprising me with small gifts: a hardcover copy of Dorothy McCarthy's *A Fool in Paradise: An Artist's Early Life*, even a ticket to a Sherlock Holmes musical. He's still the warmest man I've ever met. It sometimes occurs to me that I can enjoy feeling wronged.

I dream of Rebecca Timson. She is wearing a black taffeta dress, trimmed with lace, the one she wore the icy morning of January 11, 1864. In my dream she walks toward me, a woman in her thirties, with fine-grained white skin and gun-metal eyes. She wears an expression of unutterable calm. But she keeps her left hand in her pocket. She slowly starts to remove her hand, and I wake up with a tingling feeling down to the marrow of my bones.

Kurt pokes me in the side. In the tent, we sleep only inches away, although at home I've taken to staying up later sometimes, trying to squeeze out the time I need for my poems. Sometimes I sleep in the guest room so I won't wake him.

"What is it?" Kurt asks, but I can't tell him. The last time I spoke of Rebecca was when we planned the trip. I pointed out this place on the map, and he didn't say anything. I could actually feel him choking back his usual responses, that we wouldn't really have enough time. Then he ran his index finger along my cheek and redrew the route with a yellow marking pen, so we could cycle here and still give him time to fly to Quebec for the interview.

That night I sat down at my desk for the first time since Kurt told me that he was going after the Quebec job. I opened the third drawer and took out an oval, brass-framed photograph. The woman in the picture had a high forehead and thick dark hair pinned back in a loose bun; her eyes were piercing and she held her chin up in a determined fashion. The woman was my great-grandmother's best friend, Rebecca Timson. Then I spread out the binder where I keep the Timson poems. I wrote for hours.

We eat breakfast in camp the next morning. Then I knock on Mrs. Franklin's door. She opens it, explains that she's in the middle of carding wool and leaves me standing in the small porch. On the piano top just inside the living room I see a small brass spinning wheel, with an engraving beneath it. I step forward and read: "Master Spinner, Southern California Wool Council." Beside the spinning wheel is a photo of Mrs. Franklin standing beside a man with a recent-model General Motors station wagon. Despite his wide shoulders and open look, there's something unsettled about his expression, something rudderless.

Mrs. Franklin reappears and makes it sound as if she's doing a special favour by opening the museum. Kurt mutters that it's hardly that. According to the sign at the gate, public hours in June are 10 a.m. to 5 p.m. Tuesdays to Saturdays. Today is Wednesday, June 23.

The museum, once the home of a pioneer doctor, smells of wax and cleaning fluids. There are only two small rooms, a display area and a video room, and a backroom formerly the kitchen. Sun pours into the sepia-toned room from the side windows, scrubbed clean. I feel the press of someone's relentless energy.

The display area houses the usual registries of early gold mining claims, photographs of the town during its short heydey, an account of the Freemasons receiving their charter. But then I come across what I'm after: newspaper clippings of the mysterious stagecoach robberies and murders, Rebecca Timson's account of the young sheriff's visit to her house the night of January 10, 1864, and then the electrifying news that reached her the next morning.

Mrs. Franklin stands in the corner. I wish she would leave. Kurt studies a display of shotguns and hand pistols, while I pull out my notebook. Then I spy a facsimile of the receipt for Sheriff Plummer's coffin and burial. Something about Mrs. Franklin's lone figure compels me to reach for Kurt's hand, even though I vowed not to try to draw him into my research anymore after he made that hurtful remark in the spring. I show him the facsimile, and to my surprise he reads every word.

"Can we see the video?" I ask. I catch a hint of annoyance in Mrs. Franklin's voice.

"I'm sorry," she says. "We're in the middle of refinishing the floor there."

She seems relieved when we thank her and follow her out of the building. "Enjoy," she says. "But please don't try to get into any of the locked buildings. The state restoration people are very fussy about that."

We leave her standing on the boardwalk, watching, as we head toward the gallows on the hill back of the town. The sky is overcast this morning and the air is cool. I have an unsettling suspicion that almost nothing has changed in this valley for a hundred and thirty years.

Kurt tells me he opened the door to the video room by mistake, thinking it was a bathroom. "I didn't see any sign of refinishing a floor," he says. His voice has a thick engaged tone I haven't heard for a while. "That room was packed full of wool. Another thing. The visitor book – not written in once this month."

"Sssshhh," I say.

We follow the dirt trail into Hangman's Gulch, stopping once in a while to look back at the ghost town and to try to discern our camp spot among the poplars.

Kurt's fingers caress the back of my neck. This is a gift that is becoming rare, I realize, the gift of his active participation. I start to describe how cold it must have been the night of January 10, 1864. How in the months and weeks before, Rebecca Timson had been wakened by the sound of men arriving in whispers at her home. How one of the men had been the sheriff. And how, on the morning of January 11, Rebecca rushed to the Goodrich Hotel to be told the news. Not once does Kurt interrupt me.

The gallows are disappointing, a replica on the approximate site. I take some notes. A few drops of rain fall. At the bottom of the gulch I can see the shed where, according to the state historic map, the bodies were laid out.

Out of sight of the gallows, but towards the shed, we come across tire marks cut into the prairie. The sight makes me flinch.

"Weird place to drive," says Kurt.

I turn back to the campground. Kurt has devised a schedule to get us back to Missoula in good time, and we should leave soon. But now he says we should go on to the shed.

"You want to see it all, right?" he says.

The shed is weather-beaten and squat, one wide door and one small window, encrusted with cobwebs. I look in and see only my face, dark hair pulled back, my features more defined somehow.

The door is locked, as I have known it would be. But, like Rebecca Timson, I also have something in my pocket. I pry open the door with a chisel I picked up from behind the old blacksmith's shop. It protests gently and I peer into the blackness.

Rebecca Timson appears before my eyes. She is wearing a heavy wool coat and hand-knitted wool mitts. The body of "Dutch John" is still swinging from a protruding ridge pole, and she pushes it aside to enter. Her long skirts make a brushing sound against the dirt floor. Probably she carried a lamp. It would only have been light that morning for two hours or so. She would have been able to see her breath.

Rebecca would have walked towards the two bodies laid out on the low tables. Perhaps she spat on the sheriff's corpse, his betraying face pallid but still handsome in death. Timson, his right-hand man in the secret gang, lay beside him. Rebecca wrote in one of her verses that "greed slackened on his face." The bodies would have been stiff and frozen.

Rebecca must have known that she had only a few minutes. The vigilantes would have been busy that night. More bodies would soon be arriving.

Surely she must have closed her husband's eyes, then gone straight for his hand. The heavy gold ring would have been there, gleaming, but the fingers were tightly clenched. She pried away, but she couldn't free the ring. She must have thought it a miracle that the ring was still there. It had been fashioned by a skilful goldsmith in the town; her husband had often boasted that the ring was one of the finest examples of his craftsmanship.

Then Rebecca must have heard voices. She must have removed the hatchet from her coat pocket, and brought it down with all her force on her dead husband's wrist. She wrapped the severed hand in a piece of cloth and placed it inside her coat.

Rebecca fades away. The stanzas come flowing into my mind. And my eyes gradually make out the present-day contents of the shed. I feel Kurt's hand on my shoulder.

"Holy Jesus," he says. We stare at the new-model General Motors station wagon and a man sitting upright in the driver's seat. He doesn't move. We know right away that he never will.

Kurt moves forward, then thinks better of it.

"Looks like it happened in the last two days," he says slowly. "He seems in about the same state as a prospector my crew found up north once. Dead for two days in his cabin."

For the first time in ages I know we're thinking the same thing. Kurt and I force ourselves to walk back to the camp at a normal pace. As we approach I catch sight of a moving patch of leaf-green near our picnic table, at the same end as the stove and the water container.

Kurt and I try to loosen our bodies so the tautness of our muscles won't give us away. The figure straightens, then bends over again. When we reach camp, Mrs. Franklin has moved over to another site. She carries a garbage bag.

"Clean-up duty," she says. She makes for some dirty plastic bags in a willow bunch. She's not wearing work gloves, and I notice for the first time how well-manicured her hands are.

She moves away, picking up beer bottle caps here, bits of unburned firewood there. The wind riffles the cottonwoods.

Kurt and I strike the tent without a word, fill our water bottles from the container, pack the bicycles and cycle out of the campground. The wheels crackle on the coarse gravel.

At the top of the hill, Kurt turns back for a moment to take a drink. "We should make good time to Dillon," he says. He lifts the bottle to his lips, his square head thrown back, Adam's apple prominently outlined against the milky sky, and for a crazed instant I think I understand something about the force that compelled Rebecca Timson to sever her husband's hand. The instant passes.

"Don't drink that," I yell. I dismount and knock the bottle from Kurt's lips. Bottle and bike clatter onto the gravel.

And that's when I see it all, the images mixed up, moving and blending into each other: the vast Montana sky and the fury and betrayal on Rebecca Timson's face, her fevered plan to retrieve the one item of value within her grasp. I imagine I feel the weight of Buck Timson's stiffened hand in Rebecca's coat pocket, and the cornered fury of a woman like Ollwyn Franklin, carding and spinning away in this dark valley, alone with a husband who must have been so much less company than her spinning wheel.

Kurt's expression is hard, confused.

"What the hell did you do that for, Rebecca?" he yells back.

"You never know what she might have put in the water," I say. "She could have poisoned it while we were up at the shed. She might have guessed we'd look in."

"You might be right," Kurt says. "She had enough rat poison to kill an army."

It takes us almost two hours to make a full report at the sheriff's office.

Then we stop at the log museum in the town. I've heard there may be more photos here of the vigilantes who hanged Plummer. The museum is deserted except for one attendant, a middle-aged woman who wears blue jeans and overpowering rose cologne. Our footsteps echo on the planked floor. Saddles, cracked bridles and branding irons hang from the beams. I quickly realize there aren't any photos here that I haven't seen. We're just about to leave when I notice a tapestry on the wall.

"Nice work, isn't it?" the woman says brightly. "A local artist. Ollwyn Franklin. Prides herself on making all her own dyes, from the local grasses and flowers."

I stare at the tapestry as the woman continues. The scene, woven out of subtle greens and browns, depicts the ghost town we've just left.

Mrs. Franklin came out here from Sacramento with her husband two years before, the women tells me. People said it was her husband's idea. He retired early and loved the great outdoors.

Mrs. Franklin tried to get one of the local stores to sell her sweaters, but the townspeople hadn't shown much interest. At this point the woman sniffs. Someone else tried to get Mrs. Franklin to demonstrate spinning and carding during the local heritage days. She said she was too busy preparing for a craft show in New Mexico. Once she came to a new area, she said, she had to learn all over again how to obtain exactly the right dyes.

"Her husband seemed more approachable," the woman tells me. He'd stop and play horseshoes once in a while on trips into town. Claimed his great-grandfather used to work the mines. Last time he was in, he told the woman's husband he was thinking of moving on to Colorado.

The East Face of Sorrow Peak

She'll clear out her desk on the weekend, when only a skeleton crew will be around. But there are three more days to go, and now Vic stands in front of her, holding a scrap of paper. He's wearing the same old fuzzy brown cardigan with only one button. It occurs to Eleanor that she might actually miss all that in the new world of suits, or whatever else there is beyond these walls.

"Feel like a trip to the mountains?" Vic asks. He hands her the note.

Eleanor glances around the newsroom. She's the only one who stayed at her desk over lunch except for two summer students tapping out stories on the Klondike Days parade. After all these years she's made a rookie's mistake, hanging around this way. And it's not the only mistake she's made lately.

The note is from the night editor: "Gotta phone tip Vera Kolakiewicz (sp??) has disappeared into thin air. She's skedded to join the Cdn Everest climb in Kathmandu in a few days, rite? Better check out dayside."

Eleanor thinks how she would have jumped at this story six months ago, would already be running down the hallway for the Jasper phone book. With most rock rats, you might expect an unpredictable disappearance. But not with Vera. Vera, who'd climbed the North Face of the Eiger and the Walker Spur by the time she was twenty. Who'd been designated Climber of the Year three times by the Canadian Mountaineering Society. It was no surprise when she was named to the country's first official Everest Team, winning the chance not only to be the first Canadian but also the first North American woman to stand on the famous summit. For months the papers and television stations had been following every detail of preparation for the expedition, from training schedules to the brand of freeze-dried breakfast cereal they planned to take. Just two weeks ago Barbara Frum had interviewed Vera. She said she had never before felt as fit and ready for a major expedition.

Eleanor imagines a quiet drive through aspen forest, the cool mountain air against her cheek. Jesus, she's tired of avoiding the staff cafeteria, of explaining what she's going to do when she doesn't even know herself.

"Okay," Eleanor replies. At least in these last few days she doesn't have to carry on the charade of the past months, trying to appear enthusiastic, probably not fooling anyone. She scratches at a patch of excema that has recently started to bloom on her wrist. She never used to get these things.

"Good," says Vic. "We had Anstead do some phone checks this morning, but he didn't turn up a thing. See if you can dig up some old climbing friends, find out what's been going on in her head." He stops and looks vaguely embarrassed.

Eleanor catches a half smile on Vic's face. He'd urged her to stay. So had the editor and the managing editor. We need mature reporters, they'd said. Your experience. Your professionalism.

They couldn't understand how impossible that all seemed now. Eleanor notices, for the first time, the silver streaks in Vic's hair. He'll retire here, she thinks. She is caught off guard by the mixture of odd respect and envy the thought brings her. He'll even be more or less happy, as much as anyone ought to expect. There will be football pools and publisher's dinners and the odd downed plane or constitutional crisis to keep things lively, and the years will just go by.

Eleanor wishes she could think beyond three days. But at least she has savings to last her a while, till she figures things out.

The police radio crackles from the centre of the newsroom, where tired-looking men and women in loose sweaters or beige shirts sit around a huge U-shaped metal desk editing stories for tomorrow's paper. Vic starts to walk away, then turns back. "Could be a real barn-burner," he says.

Since she was twelve Eleanor has only wanted one thing: to be a good journalist. She thinks of this as she climbs the stairs to the newsroom library. She has never lusted for anything fancier – to be a foreign correspondent, or a columnist or a poet or novelist. She just wants to write accurate stories, to be "a skilled interpreter of the complexities of modern society," as the calendar for the journalism school had put it.

Eleanor knows exactly when she decided to become a journalist: November 22, 1963. Her social studies teacher flew into the classroom that day, declaring they would shelve Mesopotamia for forty minutes and discuss the assassination. The teacher, an English war bride with a puffy face, said no one knew yet who did it, but "they" would find out.

"They'll have to," she said. "But that's not the main question. The main question is, 'why?' Because if you can answer that one," she said, "you'll have a chance at changing things."

Figuring out the 'whys' is a lot tougher than figuring out the 'whats,' Eleanor has discovered. At first she felt terrified asking sharp-edged questions of strangers: Why is your firm clearly exceeding the regulations on effluent discharge? Why are you running for a political party that promotes sexism? But it was exhilarating too.

Eleanor sits down in front of the library reader and clicks in a cassette with clippings of climbing accidents. Her eyes don't focus on the clippings right away. Maisie Dorringer's furrowed face appears on the screen instead, and then her own face, young for its forty-one years, hair in a smooth black cap, perfectly groomed, but with something new there lately, a taut, hunted look around the eyes.

Eleanor's wrist itches. Why had she neglected to ask why that one time? Why oh why?

She walks slowly back to the newsroom, carrying a thin pile of Xeroxed clippings. Vic gestures to her. "Take Anstead with you," he says. "I don't mind going overboard on this one. You know how nuts the publisher is on anything to do with Everest."

Vic points toward one of the summer students, a particularly short-haired and well-dressed specimen from an eastern journalism school. He has a mild charm, and went out of his way to get Eleanor some Ontario contacts for a national survey story she did a few weeks ago. After the story ran, he told her he'd been amazed how many facts she could cram into one story and still make it an easy read.

Since May Eleanor has coached the students for two afternoons a week. Right away Anstead worried her, although she wasn't sure why. He's even-featured and even-limbed, with tight eyes and brittle clay-coloured hair, and has a way of stroking his chin before he speaks, as if great wisdom is about to be bestowed. He usually eats lunch at his desk, hurriedly leafing through *The Economist* and the *Canadian Review of Investigative Journalism*, instead of socializing in the cafeteria with the other reporters.

Once, when Eleanor questioned his spelling of a welfare activist's name, a man named Howard Smythe, he'd looked at her with surprise. He'd spelled the name S-m-i-t-h, couldn't be troubled to check.

"Smith can be spelled four ways," she'd told him.

"Oh," he'd said. His face was expressionless, but she'd seen the same flicker in his eyes once before, when the assignment editor asked him to cover an eggshell decoration demonstration at the Provincial Museum.

And then the same day he'd stayed late to track down ten names for that health insurance survey she'd been having trouble with. The story practically wrote itself after she got those names and phone numbers, but she hadn't known enough about the Ontario government to find her own way through that bureaucratic maze.

For nearly an hour and a half now Eleanor and Anstead have been driving almost wordlessly through the northern Alberta scrub land, where farmland gives way to aspen and then to pine.

Anstead thumbs through a file of Xeroxed clippings. Eleanor believes fiercely in being well-prepared for a story, but she still wishes he wouldn't make so much noise riffling through his papers. He seems oblivious to the rapidly changing landscape, underlining here and there, scribbling in his notebook. His writing is unusually uncontrolled, even for a journalist's, Eleanor has noted. It's all loops and the "t"s and "l"s look exactly the same.

There's something about Anstead's intensity that disturbs Eleanor, a looseness that makes her afraid. She remembers the trouble he caused with one of his first features at the paper. He'd been sent out to interview an astronomer at the university about safe ways to view the coming eclipse. A typical assignment for a summer student, fun to do, innocuous. But Anstead made a slight mistake in the dimensions the astronomer gave him for a homemade viewing box. Instead of specifying a ten-centimetre carbon filter, he'd written down "one-centimetre."

The astronomer called in near panic when the story ran. He said if anyone followed those directions and looked at the sun for more than a minute, they would suffer severe eye damage. Maybe even go blind.

Of course the paper issued a correction, but not everyone reads corrections. In ten years with the paper, no major correction has ever had to be issued as a result of Eleanor's stories. She is proud of this. On her first day on the job she'd promised herself that if she ever got careless, she'd pack it in, then and there.

Anstead looks up from the clippings.

"So you know Kolakiewicz," he says.

"I took a rock-climbing course from her a few years ago," Eleanor says. The Athabasca River is coming into view, a sheet of dull turquoise. She's glad they'll soon be in Jasper.

"Any idea what happened?," Anstead asks. "I mean, why the hell would someone who's as good a climber as she is do anything to mess up a chance at Everest?"

He has turned now, faces her. She catches a black flash in his eyes. He's gripping his Bic pen like a dagger.

"No idea," Eleanor says.

Five years ago she'd driven up the same road, all the way to the Ottertail Valley, to take a weekend climbing course. Vera stood at the bottom of the practice slabs, greeting the novice climbers with a tight handshake. She was tall, lean and muscled, with a quick smile and hair that hung in two long brown plaits. She smelled of wood smoke and sweat and her skin had the glow of physical energy.

That summer she'd scaled some of the most difficult peaks in Western Canada: the Lotus Flower Tower, the north face of Edith Cavell, the east face of Sorrow Peak. Eleanor found this difficult to believe, because Vera didn't fit into her stereotype of a climber. Maybe it was the concern in her voice, the patience she took in explaining how to tie a double figure-eight knot properly, or attach a carabiner. A pro, Eleanor thought. Here is a real pro.

Right away Vera had gathered them around the base of the slabs, pointed out tiny quarter-sized knobs and lichen-filled cracks. Then she'd looked at Eleanor and said: "You be my shadow."

Unroped, Vera sprinted up on the limestone slab, about two metres above the ground. The rock looked almost as smooth as fresh-poured paint. She completed a graceful lateral traverse in her rubber-soled shoes, moving with a ballerina's nimbleness. Eleanor, as instructed, followed her progress on the ground. She kept her feet planted the width of her hips and her arms extended to break a fall.

In less than five minutes, Vera hopped down, having completed a traverse half the length of a city block. "So now you guys practise," she said. "But always protect yourself. Have a shadow if you're not roped up."

Eleanor found herself appointed Vera's shadow for the day, partly because she'd requested an interview in advance. She learned a lot about Vera, how she'd become a nurse, hated it, run away to Australia for four years, come back to the resort town of Jasper to be a chambermaid, and one day accepted a friend's invitation for an easy climb up at the Ottertail Valley slabs.

After a group of inexperienced climbers from Calgary had a close call on Mount Temple, she and her friend Wade started up a climbing institute, mostly for schools and business groups. The institute earned just enough money to keep them roped up on rock faces all summer. They were fanatical about clean climbing and clean camps, Vera said. They didn't believe in leaving bolts and pitons stuck on the rock faces, the way some climbers did.

"I was actually rather afraid of heights at first," Vera told her, as she belayed another climber attempting his first rappel. "But I decided to just put that thought away for one day. And that's what I still do. I just put the fear away for this one day. Every day."

Eleanor wrote the usual Friday Recreation Page story back in the newsroom that Sunday night. She added a brief mention of an avalanche safety course Vera wanted to start.

A few weeks later, Vera wrote back, thanking her. Eleanor has seldom spoken to her since.

Eleanor and Anstead step out into an oppressive midafternoon July heat. It's supposed to stay cool here, she thinks. A family of Japanese tourists is taking pictures by the statue of Jasper the Bear. One child has been hoisted onto the bear's shoulders and holds on for dear life. Eleanor imagines the bear shattering into a thousand pieces and all the tourists diving for a fragment of his enameled hide. But the child smiles happily and the picture is taken.

Anstead looks surprisingly fresh in the glaring light, although some ink has leaked onto his fingers. But at least he's been smart enough to wear jeans and a sweatshirt instead of his usual navy suit jacket and khaki pants. Out here, a reporter should try to blend in.

Eleanor thinks for a moment of saying something. She's heard him talking to sources on the phone in the newsroom and thinks he's too impatient. He had the potential to be the kind of journalist she most disliked, the kind she labelled a "page oner," all razz-ma-tazz and looking out for leaks. He should listen more and talk less. Probably he doesn't realize yet that a good interview is like a fragile circle, progressing by growing rapport from point to point. If the thread breaks at any point, everything collapses.

But he's already on his way. "Meet you at the pancake house in two hours," Eleanor calls.

Watching his angular figure dash into the park information office, she finds herself suddenly stricken with envy. She used to chase that hard too, before the Maisie Dorringer incident sucked her dry.

Eleanor starts at the Chamber of Commerce. No one there knows much about Vera. She kept to herself, one of them volunteers. Try Louise at the outdoor equipment store on Patricia, she suggests. Vera used to work there off and on, between climbs, before she got the climbing institute going.

But at the outdoor store Eleanor finds Louise preoccupied, sorting out a new load of day-glo climbing pants. She identifies herself, then asks if Louise knows where Vera is.

"Haven't the foggiest idea," the clerk replies. Eleanor thanks her and scurries out.

It was like this at first with Maisie. She first found Maisie's shack in a secluded spot in a city ravine in early December. This was after an anonymous woman phoned the city desk with a tip about a homeless woman living down there. The shack was made of old plywood and cardboard. Eleanor felt shocked to the marrow when she saw smoke rising from it and realized someone actually lived there in this weather. Of course she knew squatters occasionally made illegal shelters in corners of Edmonton's vast ravine system, but she'd never come across one before at this time of year.

Eleanor knocked on Maisie's door. At first no one answered, but she kept on knocking. She noticed an empty bird feeder, made out of a jam tin, on a nearby branch. Jays screeched above.

Finally a woman opened the door. She looked about seventy-five, her face a creased matrix, her body slightly hunched but lean. She wore a checked flannelette shirt and bright purple polyester pants, which gave her a gnomelike appearance, until Eleanor noticed that her ankles were bare.

"What do you want?" the woman asked, Her voice was paper-thin

"Just to talk to you for a few minutes."

The woman gave her an appraising look. "You're not from the city? Not trying to kick me out?"

"Oh no," Eleanor said, explaining that she was from the newspaper.

The woman gestured for Eleanor to enter. "I'm Maisie Dorringer," she said. "From nowhere special, as you can see."

Inside, the light was dim. The air smelled of propane and rotting banana peels. The one room was furnished with a wooden crate which served as a table, a plastic lawn chair with half a leg missing, rusted springs covered with a cotton sleeping bag, a propane lamp and a Coleman heater. Newspapers and supermarket flyers lined the floor.

"Do you stay warm enough in here?" Eleanor asked.

The woman chuckled, not unkindly. "Course not," she said. "When I get so cold I can't sleep, I just punch myself, like this." She beat her upper forearms with the opposite hand. The sound of slapped flesh made Eleanor cringe.

"What about food?" Eleanor asked. "Do you have enough?"

"Most days," Maisie said. "Except when my leg hurts too much to root around in people's garbage." She smiled. "I don't mind going without food once in a while. But I sure feel bad when the birds go hungry."

Eleanor shivered inside her Thinsulate-lined coat. "I might be able to help you," she said. "But if I did, it would mean publicity. You probably couldn't stay on here."

The woman spoke in a low voice. "I don't want to stay here, that's for damned sure. All I want is some walls thick enough to keep me warm, so I don't have to punch myself all the time. And a little balcony so I can feed my jays."

Enough of that, Eleanor thinks. Time to get on with it. She stands on Patricia Avenue, thick with tourists, looks at her list and feels parched. The sun is hot on her back and her eyes hurt. She decides to go to the pancake house early and map out a strategy.

But at the pancake house, she is lulled by the draft from the overhead fans and buys a local newspaper instead. She's read it all by the time Anstead arrives. He looks crisp and refreshed, and impatiently orders a Diet Pepsi.

"So what did you get?" she asks.

"You first," he says, and she tells him about the woman at the sporting goods store. If they go to the bar that night, she says, they'll probably dig up a lot more than they can this afternoon.

Anstead massages his chin. His voice is scratchy and full of curves. "Guy at Parks said I should talk to Louise at the sporting store too. Got there just in time to help her bring some boxes down from one of the high shelves.

"So I tell her I'm an old friend of Vera's family, from back east. Told her I'm just in town for the weekend."

Anstead looks up, like a pup waiting to be patted. Eleanor has told her students what she thinks of journalistic misrepresentation, how it's a short cut for the lazy or unprincipled, how you need to save deceptions for the times they might really matter.

"She told me she's up at the Ottertail Valley hut," Anstead continues. "You know where that is?"

Eleanor scratches her wrist. The ring of excema seems to be spreading. She's thinking hard. The Ottertail Valley hut is where Vera used to base her avalanche training classes. Probably not many people remember that; she found a more accessible site four years ago.

Anstead taps his fingers on the formica. She could refuse to go. She's in charge here. Or she could leave Anstead in town. No, Eleanor thinks, imagining him prodding around here, rooting away there.

She jangles the car keys. She feels propelled by some unseen force, but she can't put a name to it.

They head up the Icefields Parkway, rimmed with white-capped peaks. Caravans of tourist traffic crawl along, windows open, long arms hanging out, cameras extended. A herd of wapiti grazes serenely near Whistlers' campground, seemingly oblivious to the attention they are attracting.

Anstead has his notebook out and is making a list. They should assume that something happened, he says, maybe some kind of accident people don't want to talk about. They should check at the hospital and the ambulance service as soon as they get back, and talk to the Mounties again.

"Maybe Canada's female Edmund Hillary is just another drugged-out rock jock," he says. He laughs, then catches himself.

"Sorry," he says. "I guess that's not what you're hoping. Must be a little tough for you, if she's a friend. But we'd have to write it, right?"

Eleanor turns off on a dirt track just after Sunwapta Falls. The road, pitted with potholes from last week's heavy rain, climbs sharply through spruce forest. After twenty minutes they reach a chained gate. Parks Canada has also placed three large boulders across the road.

"We get the message," Eleanor says.

Like many backcountry huts, the Ottertail Valley hut cannot be reached by car. Eleanor looks at her feet, glad she had the presence of mind to pull on her old Reeboks. Anstead wears a pair of hiking shoes that look brand-new. Another rule of journalism broken: always be prepared to move fast. He'll break more rules, she thinks.

"See you up there," Eleanor says.

She leaves Anstead behind as she sprints easily along the overgrown road, which soon deteriorates into a churned-up trail used mostly by horses. She comes to a creek where an old bridge must have washed out the previous spring. Stagnant water glistens in the creek bed; Eleanor crosses on a narrow log someone has thrown across. Wonder how Anstead will enjoy this, she thinks. She hears only the sound of her own breathing and the odd squawk of grey jays.

The log hut sits in a clearing, facing the grey peaks of the Front Ranges. It's chinked, green-roofed, antlers above the door. There's a hitching post by the porch and corrals in the back, but no sign of horses.

The door is half open. Eleanor knocks lightly. She hears the reluctant scrape of leather soles on the planked floor, and looks up into Vera's face.

"Eleanor," she says, and shrugs. "Trust you to track me down."

Eleanor nods.

"Well, if it has to be someone, I'm glad it's you." Vera's voice is watered down, softer than ever, and her skin looks dull. The hair, which Eleanor has always seen plaited, falls over her shoulders, lank and styleless. There are dishes piled on a small wooden table, rock shoes strewn on the floor.

Vera gestures to the porch, and they sit down on wooden chairs. The paint is peeling badly. Anstead could be here any minute, Eleanor thinks, trying to keep herself from reaching for her notebook too soon.

There are times to be direct when you want a story, times to circle first. "So why the hell aren't you packing up for Kathmandu?" Eleanor says, pleasantly.

And it all comes out, in torrents, the way she's seen it happen before, usually with people who have experienced grief, or trauma, and she feels the same old shock, the way her media ID opens up the world to these intimate chambers. She knows, in a way, that Vera has been waiting for her, or someone like her, all this time. She even knows that she is fulfilling a function that has nothing to do with page one.

"I can't cut it," Vera is saying. She paints a word picture for Eleanor, tells how five days ago she'd gone for a climb with her friend Wade. They chose the east side of Sorrow Peak, because it would be challenging enough to be interesting. Vera took the lead and Wade followed.

Maybe it was the excitement of the impending trip, maybe she was overtired. She got halfway up the fourth pitch. There she found herself in a chimney that was blocked by a basketball-sized boulder jammed between the quartzite walls.

"Of course I should have tested the hold before I committed to it," she says. "Of course I should have. Golden rule of climbing, and I totally ignored it."

The boulder held for only a moment, then broke loose. Vera remembers a shriek and a flash of grey as she dropped into space. But her protection held. She fell about five metres and then the rope tightened, caught by the cam device placed just before the fall. She managed to climb onto a small ledge, arms scraped and bleeding, but otherwise unhurt.

Then she heard Wade moaning softly from the spot below where he'd been belaying her. With one hand he was clutching his head. That's when Vera knew where the shriek came from. The boulder had struck Wade on his forehead below his helmet.

She called out to him but he didn't answer, and his body seemed to slump. "He had a concussion and passed out," Vera says. "Thank God it was only a few minutes. I was able to help him get down to the bottom of the face and then I ran to our camp for a sleeping bag and a tent. He moaned all night, but seemed better in the morning, and said I mustn't worry and that you've got to expect something like this once in a while. He's resting at his dad's place out on the coast now. But think what could have happened."

She pauses, looks straight at Eleanor. "Do you have to write up all this? The publicity could kill the institute. I can live without the climb, but I depend on the institute."

Eleanor doesn't answer. Vera shrugs again, leans forward, hugs herself. "What a sandbagger, eh? So how could I still even think about going up Everest?"

From the edge of the clearing Eleanor sees Anstead's figure approaching. He is limping.

For the first time since the Dorringer incident, Eleanor is certain how to proceed.

"Deal?" she says. "You do what I ask you the next five minutes. And we'll deal."

Vera doesn't say anything but she doesn't argue. It's as if she's in Eleanor's hands, giving her complete authorial freedom to write or rewrite her story. Eleanor grabs the rock shoes.

The two women rush along a shrubby path through a grove of white spruce to the bottom of the Ottertail Valley slabs. Eleanor hands Vera the rock shoes.

"Here," she says. "I'll shadow you."

And Vera's up on the slabs, slow-footed at first, her right leg searching for a toehold with the care of a butterfly looking for exactly the right flower to land on. She finds the toehold and then she's sailing, long thin arms and legs gliding as easily as if she were walking along a garden path. Eleanor follows along beneath her, grounded, ready to break a fall.

In eight minutes Vera reaches the edge, hops down.

"Some sandbagger," Eleanor says.

"The first minute, I couldn't move on that rock," Vera says, as they walk quickly back to the hut.

"But you got over it," says Eleanor.

"Yes," says Vera. "I got over it."

Just before they reach the hut, Eleanor turns.

"Why me? Why did you tell me?"

Vera plucks a wild rose, puts it behind her ear.

"You know that blurb you did on avalanche safety? That kicked off the whole program, opened the doors for me to get some funding for the institute."

They are nearly at the hut. Eleanor turns and looks back at Vera. "I won't be able to keep it out of the papers forever, you know."

She nods. "But you can for a few days. Time to figure this all out myself, instead of having the media decide it for me."

They return to the front porch. Anstead is sitting on the chair, his pants spattered with mud up to his knees, his right sock and shoe off. "You didn't tell me we'd be bushwacking," he says.

When he sees Vera, his expression changes. He reaches for his notebook, but by then Eleanor is pulling him away.

"I've got everything," she says. "We've gotta hustle."

She flies back to the car, feeling the trail and the spruce forest and the sky blending into one. She sees Maisie in front of her, the Maisie her story created, the Maisie who appealed for help, for food and something more than plywood walls. And she sees the envelopes pouring in from all over the city, some rolls of five-dollar bills, rolled up loonies from school children, elegantly written cheques from oil companies. In all, an incredible twenty-five thousand dollars.

She sees herself presenting the cheque to Maisie in front of the Christmas Tree in Winston Churchill Square. A band started to play "Good King Wenceslas" and television cameras from every station whirred. Then she wrote the story; it appeared on page one with full colour the next day. A particularly caustic radio talk show host, known for his feuds with the paper, said he had to admit that it had really caught the spirit of Christmas this time.

And then six weeks ago the call from Simon, a reporter friend at a newspaper on the coast, saying he'd been going through back issues and seen the story.

"You fell for Greedy Gretta," he says. "Welcome to the club. She's already pulled that stunt in Toronto and Vancouver."

Later, when Eleanor checked back in the library files, she found it – a headline and picture of Maisie, under the name of Gretta but easily recognizable. It was all there, if only she'd taken the trouble to look more than one year back in the files.

By the time anyone thought to call the police, Gretta and the twenty-five thousand were nowhere to be found.

It's almost dark by the time Eleanor and Anstead arrive back in the city. Eleanor has already composed her lead in her head: "Renowned Jasper climber Vera Kolakiewicz says she will likely join the Canadian Everest expedition in Kathmandu later this week.

"Contrary to some reports, she at no time had serious plans to abandon the climb. However, the 34-year-old climber admitted in an exclusive interview Wednesday that she daily struggles with a fear of heights."

Nowhere in the story will there be mention of unsafe climbing practices.

After all, we're only human, Eleanor thought. People make mistakes. Even the best of us occasionally give a rope too much play, or place our faith in a hold that turns out to be rotten.

In the newsroom parking lot, she opens the trunk of her car and hands Anstead his bag. He points at his feet. "Won't make that mistake again," he says. He grins and shrugs his shoulders. She surprises herself by managing a smile.

Only a couple of reporters linger in the newsroom, cleaning up from dayside. Eleanor hears the static from the police radio and the hum of the newsroom printer and it comes to her that she feels at home. Somebody has to keep an eye on the Veras and the Grettas and, of course, the Ansteads of this world.

Outside Interests

Wendell Stephenson, Landscape Painter, age forty-four

I can't honestly say I noticed anything unusual about them at first. To tell you the truth I was pretty wrapped up in my work up there. It was the second week of Indian summer in the Rockies. At noon the air would be so warm I'd strip down to my waist painting; by evening dinner could start freezing on your fork before you got it into your mouth.

I'm exaggerating, of course, but that's what the back country around Banff is like this time of year and that's why I go up there for five or six days. Everything can be so intense one moment, the sky so damn blue your eyes practically pop and the larches bright as oranges, and the next minute it can be snowing like a son-of-a-bitch. A watercolourist like me can end up with wet-in-wet techniques he never in a million years could have planned, and half the time the result isn't half bad.

I got into camp late the afternoon the Parlburgs arrived. That would have been a Monday. Of course I didn't know their names then. The campground isn't much, no picnic tables, just a few fire grates, pit toilets and flattened areas of hard dirt to pitch a tent on. It's a day's walk in from the highway and that discourages the amenities. There were only two campsites that appealed to me, because they were right by a stream and had a striking view of Empress Mountain. The other sites were back in the bush. Just like National Parks to stick campers back there.

Naturally I'd chosen one of the view sites; I seemed to be the only camper around except for an old guy who disappeared that morning with his fishing tackle. He'd taken one of the back sites. God knows why.

I'd set up my camp and got a little fire going in the grate when the Parlburgs arrived. I didn't say hello; socializing isn't big on the minds of most of the people who go up there.

They were both tall, in their mid-forties, I'd say. They carried big packs with climbing ropes and ice axes sticking out the top. The man had a full beard, neatly trimmed, and looked to me to be a little on the heavy side. When he swung his pack down he already seemed to surveying the ground for optimum tent placement. He had the demeanor of a physics prof, I thought, precise and controlling, although later I found out that he was a geologist with a struggling consulting business in forestry-related data bases. The woman had short blond hair, a high brow and rather a distracted but capable air about her. She impressed me at the time as the kind of woman who insists on doing half the driving because she thinks it's only fair, then drives you crazy by making a complete stop at every intersection whether she needs to or not.

That evening I was engrossed in a new biog of Winslow Homer. All the same I could hear the rustling sounds of a tent and sleeping bags being pulled out of packs, the clank of cooking pots and the click of aluminum poles connected by shock cords snapping together to form the skeleton of the tent. I have a similar tent; up to then I'd found comfort in that sound.

"Damn," the man's voice said, punching into the calm. "I told you not to do that. Push, don't pull."

"What?"

"The cord's snapped apart inside its sleeve. That's because you were pulling it. If we're not careful, we'll rip the nylon."

"It's all right," the woman said, her tone flat. "I can fix it. My hands are smaller."

"No, no. I've got it."

There were a few minutes of silence, then the man exclaimed. "Shit," he said. "The cord's torn apart."

"I can fix it," the woman replied. "I brought a sewing kit."

"Get me a needle and some thread," the man replied.

I found a spot closer to the stream. I might even have moved to one of the back sites, except by this time another hiker, a young woman, had arrived and claimed the best one.

I should have made my own camp in the woods, I thought. Already the campground was getting too crowded.

Bob Shanks, Fisherman, retired civil servant, age sixty-five

I went up there for peace and quiet, not the circus it turned out to be. For the first few days, though, I was happy enough. The weather was holding and I couldn't complain about the fishing. The hours just go by like lightning for me as long as I have a rod in my hand, and I was having pretty good luck with a wet fly. I was after a fight and that's what I got from those rainbows. Sometimes it was like having a torpedo on your line.

I forced myself to catch and release, even though it's not what I'm accustomed to. You have to change with the times, I tell myself. Still it hurt to hold one of those beauties in my hand, splashing water against its gills, and feel it coming back to life. For a moment it made the whole day seem pointless, just like being retired can seem pointless if I think too much about it.

Company was not what I went up there for, so I have to admit I was not entirely happy when I went back up to the lake just after supper and found that woman there. Not that she wanted to be intrusive. But something bothered me about it at the time, and later too, although I still haven't put all the parts together.

She was good-looking, although that doesn't show up on television. You could see spidery veins on her nose and cheeks; it was the kind of face that liked the sun.

When I got up to the lake, which was about twenty minutes' walk from the campground, Mrs. Parlburg was sitting on a rock near my favourite fishing spot. She had her knees drawn up, balancing a cooking pot. I realized she was eating her dinner alone, which seemed a little strange because I'd seen her come into the campground with a big fellow I assumed was her husband. But it wasn't my business. Myself, I like to eat outdoor meals alone. That's why I took a back site at the campground.

Something about my expression must have jarred Mrs. Parlburg, because she started to move off the rock as soon as she saw me.

"It's all right," I said. "I'll go on the other side."

I thought she looked a bit surprised, and grateful too. I'm not like some, I know I don't own the park. Not like that artist fellow, scowling like the blazes when I took a short cut through his site. We all have an equal right to this park, but only if we appreciate it.

The weather was still holding, although all hell broke out later that week. The lake was calm, except for quicksilver rings and ripples where the fish jumped. Empress Mountain reflected back in its waters. It was pretty as a picture.

She came up behind me just as I was releasing the third catch of the night. A pretty little rainbow, speckled and gleaming. I pulled the hook out of the rainbow's mouth and then moved her back and forth in the lake, swishing water in her gills. I could feel Mrs. Parlburg's eyes on me all that time. I don't mind saying it made me a tad uncomfortable.

"Don't you mind letting them go?" she asked.

"No," I said, although I could tell by the way she tilted her head, amused-like, that she didn't believe me.

"It's the catch that counts," I said. "It's only when you haven't made a catch that letting go sounds so bad."

"My husband used to take my son out fishing," she said. "I never had the patience myself."

"How old is your son?" I asked, mostly to be polite. I have a teen-age grandson myself; the only fishing he's interested in is for spending money.

"Fourteen," she said.

"So he doesn't want to go out fishing anymore with the old man?"

"No," she said. Her lips were pursed tight and she wouldn't take her eyes off the spot where I had released the fish.

"The boy would love to," she finally said. "It's Bernard. He thinks the fishing wouldn't be so good if he brought the boy along. He thinks he'd be too noisy and restless."

I didn't know what to say, so I just kept casting and reeling.

Finally the woman said, in a light, merry tone: "He's probably right."

Then she walked back to the camp. I caught and released two more rainbow before I called it a day. But it wasn't getting any easier, letting them go.

What was the point of the day, I wondered when I got back to camp. What really was the point?

Patricia Rabik, Graduate Student in Biology, age twenty-five

I hate to play a know-it-all and say, yes, I knew there was something freaky about that couple. But it's true that something twigged for me. I was up early that Tuesday morning, because I wanted to hike to Giant's Toe. The Parlburgs were just breaking camp. It was about 6 a.m. Actually, it was kind of a late start for a climb. And for sure that's what they planned to do. They were leaving the tent behind, though. I figured they were going up the South Ridge of Empress Mountain in one day and planned to be back by nightfall. I felt mildly curious about their chances of success, since they were no spring chickens. I had a boyfriend in my undergraduate years who climbed a bit and he tried that route once. He took a nasty fall and almost swore off climbing. I remember telling him he could learn something about longevity from male bighorns.

"The vigorous males with the large horns hardly ever live past fifteen years," I told him. "It's the smaller-horned, less aggressive ones that live to twenty-four years. Funny, isn't it? I have a research paper on that somewhere."

"You're telling me the dominant ram pays a price for success?" my boyfriend asked.

"Something like that," I said.

He didn't seem impressed.

By the time I got going that Tuesday, it was after 8 o'clock. My plan was to hike up the west flank of Empress Mountain to the toe. It really does look like a giant's toe in the distance, the way it slopes down to a huge boulder that's sort of flat on top, like somebody's toenail, and the rest is rounded. I'm not a climber myself, I prefer hiking, which is part of the reason why I picked the maternal behavioural patterns of bighorn sheep as my thesis topic. But I wasn't really thinking about my thesis on that trip; I was hiking to get away from it.

I didn't meet any other hikers that day, although I did notice footprints. About halfway up the mountain the trail split off to the South Ridge, and the footsteps ended.

The day was warm and bright, and I made the toe in good time. For a while I lay in the sun, watching some mountain sheep graze along the base of the mountain. On the way down I started to develop a blister but I figured I'd make it to camp okay.

What surprised me is that I ran into the Parlburg woman. This would have been about 4 o'clock. Actually, I thought her husband was ahead of her at the time, so I didn't think too much about it.

The woman was sitting beside a stream, not far from the trail. She had her boots off and was washing her feet. Her hair caught the sun and looked gold and silver, and when she saw me she waved. I hadn't talked to anyone all day so I thought, what the hell, and I sat down beside her.

"And what have you seen today?" she asked.

I told her about the toe, and the mountain sheep.

When I asked her about the climb, she replied flatly that it had been unsuccessful and that they would try again tomorrow.

All that time she had her feet in the stream. The water looked refreshing and I took off my boots too and stuck my feet in. The water was so cold I almost screamed.

"How can you stand it?" I asked.

She laughed. "They go numb after a while," she said. "It's healing, actually."

I became aware that she was looking at the soles of my feet.

"You have a blister developing," she said.

"Yes, I know," I said.

"Then you should do something about it," she said. "The minute you know you have a blister is the time to attend to it."

She actually insisted on treating the blister herself. I couldn't help noticing how comprehensive her first aid kit was. She even had folding scissors and a pair of panty hose which she said was for holding a compress in place in an emergency.

"That's much better," I said. "Are you a nurse?"

She shook her head. "Occupational therapist, actually, but that was mostly because I like mucking about with paint and am cursed with a practical nature! But right now I'm not working."

She was spending quite a bit of time with her son, she said, setting up a home study program with him this term.

"I introduced him to oil paints last year. He really caught the bug. Now he wants to quit hockey and basketball and just paint all the time."

We walked back to the campground together.

"Tell me more about the mountain sheep," she said. We were both tired and happy enough to have company.

"They desert their young," I remembered. "If they're both in danger, Mom says 'Bye-bye.'"

The woman, who said her name was Sharon, shuddered. "How terrible," she said.

"Actually," I said, "it makes sense biologically. If a bear, say, gets Mom, it'll also get Junior. If only Junior bites the dust, Mom can breed again within the year."

"Nonetheless, how terrible."

The next day I woke up to rain and sleet, so I went back down. I never saw Sharon again, although like everyone else I've been following the story in the papers.

Wendell Stephenson

I had a superb painting day Tuesday. My goal for the trip was to paint the mountain from four perspectives, but always at the same elevation. Next year maybe I'll get a few more. Who knows, maybe in five or ten years, I'll be satisfied that I've captured this mountain from all the best perspectives. That'd be something worth striving for.

I was away from the campsite all Tuesday and went straight into the tent when I got back. When I woke up on Wednesday morning it was raining like the devil. Good thing I came prepared – solid plastic grips for the completed paintings and a packful of plastic bags. When the sound of rain on the fly softened I unzipped the tent door and saw snow, large chunky flakes. There wasn't any sign of activity at the Parlburg's tent, but I heard the young girl at the back site packing up.

The hell with it, I thought. I deserve a day off. I knew the snow would melt soon enough. I went back to sleep and stayed in the tent most of the day, reading a bit and doing some sketching. From time to time I thought I heard voices in the next tent, but that may have been the sound of the pines shaking off snow.

In late afternoon the snow stopped, the wind calmed down and the sun actually came out for a while. I cooked supper early, planning on getting up before sunrise the next day.

I was sitting on a seat made of a sawed-off tree trunk and sipping instant coffee when a woman's voice said, "Hello. Are we the only ones left in the campground?"

"I'm not sure. That fisherman is probably knee deep in a lake," I said. "He probably hasn't even noticed it's raining."

The woman introduced herself. Sharon. A pretty name, I thought. She was clutching a cup of coffee herself and wore a rag wool toque that had about the same mixture of white and black as her hair.

I motioned to another tree trunk chair. Sharon pulled one over. She had a lithe, strong way of moving that reminded me of TV portrayals of army nurses.

"You're an artist," she said. "Do you mind if I ask you something?"

Then she asked if I had taken special training as a child, what had helped me the most, the usual. I don't remember the details.

"Are you interested in art yourself?" I asked.

She pushed her hair back from her face. "Not so much now," she said. "I used to have a little studio at home, but one day an intruder broke into the house and trashed it. Smeared oil paints all over the walls. I never had the heart to go at it again."

"That's terrible."

"Well, it's the boy I'm thinking about now. He wanted to enroll in a fine arts high school this year."

"Sounds like a good idea," I said.

"His father did not agree," Sharon said.

"And you?"

"I enrolled him anyway."

"Good for you."

"Not really. His father disenrolled him."

"Ah."

I was beginning to feel drawn into something that did not appeal to me.

"Going down soon?" I asked. A light drizzle had started again.

"Tomorrow," Sharon said.

We said good night shortly after. I heard not a sound from the tent all night.

The next day, the Thursday, dawned bright and clear. I decided to go up the South Ridge trail on the other side of Empress Mountain, as far as I could without climbing. I wanted to get a close-up perspective, and there probably wouldn't be many more opportunities. Snow was already at least a hundred feet lower on the base than a few days before.

As soon as I took the fork toward the South Ridge, the trail became much steeper and more indistinct. My breath hung in misty puffs.

It wasn't long before the trail petered out in front of a smooth limestone wall. I have never had the urge to climb, but for a moment I wished I could. I could imagine the satisfaction of finding solid toeholds and footholds. Yet I have to admit that I found something disturbing about the area. Above that first wall of limestone the slope receded into a dark, rock-strewn gully. There must have been boulders as big as an automobile up there. Even as I watched, a small rockfall high up on the ridge rumbled down the steep slopes.

I decided not to linger. Instead I hiked straight down, to a rather pretty unnamed lake, and got a few new perspectives on the mountain. Once or twice I thought I heard a voice calling from somewhere up on the South Ridge, but guessed it was probably the wind.

Later on, as I was packing up, I saw a flash of green at the bottom of the limestone wall. I was curious enough to fetch my binoculars, and was rather surprised to see Sharon Parlburg up there. But I didn't think much about it. People have the right to change their minds.

Later that afternoon, when the helicopter set down in the meadow near the campground and all the questions began, I didn't really have much to say.

What I want to know is, what kind of an intruder would take the time to smear oil paint over someone's walls?

Bob Shanks

Sure, I was the one who notified the wardens. But that woman, Sharon, tipped me off. See, she came up to the lake again on Wednesday night. It had snowed like hell all day but what did I care, I had enough gear to stay as dry as the Dead Sea scrolls.

Actually, I was happy enough to see her. That wet snow can get you down; the chill penetrates so bad. All day the clouds were wrapped tight as wads of cotton batten around the base of Empress Mountain. You'd hardly even know there was a mountain there.

The woman provided a bit of colour. Know what I mean? She had that glossy green anorak on, and her face shone from the mist and, I think, sun and wind burn.

"Still catching and releasing?" she asked. She seemed amused, as one is with a child who continues at a pointless game.

"You bet," I said.

"Do you think you're catching the same fish?" she asked.

I told her I thought that was very likely.

"I read an article about a study on trout around here," she said. "Someone examined their mouths. They found one fish that had been caught and released forty-two times. Imagine."

"Pretty dumb, eh? " I said.

"Yes," she said. "But it's sad, too, don't you think? I mean, that they don't learn? That they're still drawn to the same bait?"

I suppose you could think of it like that, I said.

"What would make them stop, do you think?" she asked.

"Oh, that's easy," I said. "Being caught and not being released. That would certainly teach them a thing or two."

"Oh yes," she said, in a cheerful tone. "I am sure it would."

"Did your husband go down?"

"Last night."

Of course then I knew she was lying. I'd seen her with her husband early Tuesday morning, heading up the trail to the South Ridge, and later I watched with my binoculars as they gained the ridge. They looked as small as ants. You can't tell me someone would go up that ridge and back down to the highway the same day.

I went down myself that night. It was the last trip of the season. Right now I don't even want to think about fishing. What would it be like, I wonder, to be caught and released, over and over again?

Patricia Rabik

All I wanted to do that Thursday night was to be a complete couch potato. I got the laundry done, the grit out of my hair, came out of the shower in bare feet, towel wrapped around me, and flicked on the TV.

Well, you could have knocked me over with a feather. The 6 p.m. news, and the announcer going crazy. Images of a helicopter swooping down near a campground, circling around a mountain, people yelling, screaming. A haggard-looking man lying on a stretcher, then disappearing into the helicopter.

And then the camera zooms in on Sharon, you know how they do? She looked right at the camera too, as if daring it to come closer.

And then the reporter, practically breathless:

"Wardens today rescued a 45-year-old Calgary businessman who had fallen while climbing the South Ridge of Empress Mountain Tuesday. The man, Bernard Parlburg, had apparently broken his leg in a fall from South Ridge into a steep gully. He claims that his wife kept him supplied with food, water, first-aid equipment and warm clothing, but had made no attempt to rescue him, and he was not able to rescue himself."

I flicked off the TV. My hands were trembling and I didn't trust myself to stand up. Then I noticed that the moleskin Sharon put on my heel on Tuesday had almost peeled off. I pulled the rest off. Looks like Sharon was right. The blister is all healed.

Wendell Stephenson

I decided to stay on despite all the excitement. Some new campers appeared on Friday with stories that made my hair stand on end. Next year I'll definitely have to find a new camp.

Indian summer came back that Saturday, the sky bright blue and most of the snow gone. A few larches clung to their needles, which had faded by that time. Empress Mountain stood out so clearly against that brilliant sky that it almost looked like a different mountain. There were ridges and buttresses high up that I'd never noticed before. When I went back to look at the paintings I'd done earlier that week, I found them wan and unconvincing. Up to then, they had pleased me.

The Language of Aggression

The music has started up again. Maretta can't make out the lyrics, but she feels the vibrations thudding deep in her skull. She thinks it sounds like a pack of weasels rioting, and wonders if she's been teaching English too long.

She places her pen down on the picnic table. The surface is satisfyingly clean, no carved initials or chipped paint. Someone left a medium-sized pile of split wood beside the firepit. The campsite is perched a few metres above the braided silty channels of the Mistaya River, beneath a bower of lodgepole pine, spruce and fir. The rushing water drowns out the whirr of traffic on the Icefields Parkway, a chain of speeding steel and rubber stretching on this holiday weekend from Lake Louise to Jasper. Across the river, the Rockies rise almost vertically to the Continental Divide, catching the faint alpenglow of the August evening.

Now she can make out the lyrics. They are bullying their way into her eardrums, drowning out the sound of water rushing over stone.

My mouth is dry, my heart is hurtin',
With the other guys you're always flirtin'.

The music comes from the only adjacent site, where a white and green-trimmed South Wind RV with bruised B.C. plates drove up an hour ago. Maretta hadn't noticed much else at the time. She'd been too busy trying to finish marking. If she could just get Jacqueline van Heeckeren's interminable essay out of the way, she thought, she could start to enjoy the weekend.

I've got a chain around my neck,
Sixty links to hold me down.
You say you love me twice as much
While you kick me on the ground.

For a moment Maretta imagines pulling the Swiss Army knife out of her daypack and plunging it into the South Wind's tires. They look like they've seen better days anyway.

A slight breeze blows off the river and feels ice-fresh against her cheek. She studies the eighteen-page, single-spaced paper in front of her. The essay is called "The Day I Discovered Jenny's Green Tomato Pickles," and gives a relentlessly detailed account of a shopping excursion to the Strathcona Farmers' Market in Edmonton. Jacqueline is one of the most determined students in Maretta's advanced English as a Second Language class. She's about forty-five, ten years older than Maretta, and recently emigrated from Rotterdam. A chubby woman with dry flaked skin and round, demanding blue eyes and a nervous drive that Maretta both respects and dislikes. She's always late for class, always the first to hand in her assignments.

Jacqueline has already called twice to see if she can discuss her essay, even though Maretta told the class she'd need a week to mark them all. But Maretta had found herself promising to have Jacqueline's essay back on Tuesday morning, three days early, even if that meant packing it along on this trip.

Ten years a teacher, she thinks, and I still let them do this to me. Jesus. Her friend Anna, who teaches the other section, would never do that. She knows the other teachers have nicknamed them "The Meek and Mild" and "The Antsy and Wild." Anna even manages to put her foot down whenever The Turtle tries to get her to increase her student-teacher ratio. The Turtle is Maretta's nickname for the college administrator, a short-necked, apple-cheeked woman named Etta Mueller. What usually happens is that Maretta gets stuck with the extra student instead. That's how she got Jacqueline.

In large block letters, Jacqueline has printed: "I wanted to buy some pickels at the market."

Maretta circles "pickels," then puts her pen down. Someone has turned up the music again, a wall of noise.

You can't make me love you
You can't make me hurt you anymore
You can't say you're sorry cause I'm walking out the door.

She places the essay back in the cheap vinyl folder that Jacqueline provided, then stands and shakes the dust off her tailored cotton drill shorts and walks toward Site 54G. A black ghetto-blaster sits on the picnic table. No one seems to be about.

"Excuse me," Maretta calls, then knocks on the door.

A young woman answers. She looks about twenty-five, with loose brown hair and carefully applied eyeliner, and she wears a two-piece lime bathing suit. Sand clings to the woman's kneecaps, as if she's been messing in a sand pile and didn't have the energy to clean herself.

"Would you mind turning down your music a bit?" Maretta asks, hating herself for adding "a bit."

The woman looks at her as if she had asked her to jump in the lake.

"Just a bit?" Maretta repeats. She smiles brightly. A trusted emollient, that smile. She sometimes wishes that she could start over in life, throw away that smile, be the sort of person who cruises through amber lights, who wears sequined tops and isn't fanatical about keeping old *New Yorkers* shelved in exact chronological order. More like Anna.

The woman shrugs.

"It's not that loud," she says. Her voice is thin and neutral, and when she speaks she reveals a chipped front tooth. She throws a cigarette stub on the ground and shuts the door.

Maretta walks back to her site. It's only seven-thirty. The music, if anything, seems louder. She hears shouts from the woods behind her, more people streaming into the park from their offices in Calgary and Edmonton, wrestling with their tents, chopping wood. The other sites would probably be taken by now. She should consider herself lucky.

What was it the girl at the kiosk had said when she drove in? "Oh, you'll love Site 53G. You can see the tip of Mt. Chephren from there."

The girl had a slick black ponytail and even teeth, and was dressed in the drab khaki uniform of Parks Canada. She wore a brass pin with "Jeanne" printed on it.

"I'm giving a talk on bears tonight, in the fire circle," Jeanne said. "Why don't you come?"

Maretta just nodded. For some reason, she didn't want to disappoint the young woman by telling her that she'd already attended several such talks, and figured that by this time she knew all she needed to know about bears. What Maretta desperately wanted, she told Jeanne, was to see the Rocky Mountain wildflowers in bloom.

The word "desperately" just slipped out, and Maretta looked up anxiously to see if Jeanne found anything odd about it. If she had, she didn't show it. Oh well, Maretta thought, it was true. Her nerves did feel shaved, desperate.

"You've come at exactly the right time," Jeanne smiled, pencilling in several appealing trails on a simplified Parks Canada map. "Hope you have at least three days!"

Maretta imagined purple-hued meadows full of silky lupine, cool grassy circles where Indian paintbrush and yellow ragwort bloomed for just a few weeks in glorious seclusion, where arnica and asters and globeflower created a wonderful crazy-quilt bordered by soaring peaks. She'd just get the goddamned essay out of the way and then she could start enjoying things.

When she planned the trip, she read in a guidebook that Mary Schäffer, an early explorer to the Canadian Rockies, had loved the area – its lakes and butterflies and ground squirrels and chipmunks and ducks and beavers and flowers. "No ripple of worry from the outside could touch us," she had written.

Lucky Mary, Maretta thinks. She places the essay back into her Vuitton briefcase and locks it in the trunk. Once Anna put her students' papers in the back seat of her antique Thunderbird when she went to a symposium in Calgary. The papers blew out the window and scattered all over the highway. One of the students got a telephone call a few days later from a pensioner who found the young man's homework lying by a ditch near Bowden.

Where Maretta grew up, on a farm in Saskatchewan, there weren't stereos or ghetto-blasters. There weren't even neighbours, at least not nearby. On Sunday evenings, her soft-spoken parents would bring out an old phonograph and play 33 r.p.m. records, mostly Patti Page and Frank Sinatra, sometimes *The Goldberg Variations* or *Seventeenth Century English Music for Viol and Keyboard.* The phonograph was placed on the mahogany table in the farmhouse living room, with its paisley-patterned linoleum floor and doily-covered end tables. In summer months, Maretta went to sleep to the sound of frogs croaking in the sloughs behind the barn.

Some of the town kids at school lived in houses with broadloomed carpets and hi-fis. But Maretta never recalled feeling deprived. That came later, in cinder block apartments in the city, with the sound of footsteps overhead, or someone else's car radio blasting through her bedroom windows. Then she began to feel that she had indeed been deprived, that she lacked some essential psychic armour that city people possessed that helped them live near each other. She hadn't figured out what that armour was made of, only that people like Anna and Jacqueline possessed it, and she didn't.

She presses her hands against the cool metal of the Toyota, and hears a faint strain of music from another corner of the campground. Someone is playing early Cat Stevens.

You're such a snob, Anna told her once. They were driving to the beach in Anna's Thunderbird, and she turned down the volume on the tape, by The Dead Kennedys, or the Fried Parrots, or something equally outrageous.

"If I was playing Mozart that loud, you wouldn't complain," Anna had said.

Were, Maretta wanted to say. If you *were* playing Mozart. But she held back. It wasn't that she was exceptionally disciplined at holding her tongue, as some of the other teachers at the college surmised, or even that she was especially kind. It was just that, since the age of ten, she could never will herself to throw out words the way most people did, words that could cut, or command, or defend.

One day, the year Maretta was ten, her cousin Linda came out from town to spend the day. Maretta had shown her the special place by the creek, where tiger lilies bloomed, and Linda had pulled up a handful by the roots. Maretta ran screaming into the house, calling her a bitch. It was a word she'd heard the hired man use, when he thought he was alone.

Maretta's mother had slapped her, hard, on the cheek.

"The lilies," Maretta cried. "Linda pulled tiger lilies by the roots."

When you come home by four
I know you've been with him
You good for nothing woman
I'm not gonna take it any more.

Maretta feels her chest weaken, then remembers what Jeanne said, about an interpretive program that night in the fire circle. Anything would be better than this, she thinks.

She walks down the gravel road, past large RVs and tents shaped like mushrooms. A few campers sit around picnic tables, or on webbed lawn chairs. She doesn't hear any other music, not even Cat Stevens.

The fire circle has been hacked out of a stand of mixed spruce. About two dozen sawed-off tree trunks, makeshift seats, are assembled in a circle. Jeanne sits in the centre, cross-legged on a blanket between two large boxes. One box is labelled "Dynamite" in large block letters. The other box is labelled "A Sack of Goose Feathers, So to Speak."

Eight people are seated around the circle, including a moon-faced man and three small children with sticky-looking faces and sour expressions. The mother, who has short black hair in a geometric cut, smiles wanly at Maretta. She wonders if she should sit down beside them, but suddenly imagines a sticky hand grasping at her legs. She nods and takes a seat directly opposite.

Jeanne smiles, looks at her watch and says: "Too late, too bad."

She flashes a conspiratorial smile and pulls a huge brown hide out of the box labelled "Dynamite." Maretta cringes inwardly at the sight of the dead beast's claws.

Then Jeanne lifts a thick black hide out of the box marked "Sack of Goose Feathers, So to Speak."

She smiles again. "Fooled you, eh? In case you want to know the difference between a grizzly bear and a black bear, this just about sums it up. At least, according to Andy Russell."

Jeanne lifts the grizzly claws up to her face so everyone can get a good look. The claws stretch from her eyebrow clear down to her mouth. Maretta imagines what it must be like to be at the top of the food chain, instead of being a teacher at the mercy of administrators and nagging students.

The theme of the talk is how to avoid bear trouble by understanding bear habitat and needs. Maretta listens with more interest than she expected, considering she's heard most of it before. Not all black bears are black, the naturalist is saying, and not all grizzlies are brown. They can also be cinnamon and black.

"How many of you have seen grizzlies in the park?" Jeanne asks.

All the members of the family across from Maretta raise their hands. She feels somehow left out by this revelation.

Bears are a lot like people in some ways, Jeanne is saying. They use facial features and their ears to convey aggression.

Maretta likes the way Jeanne talks about bears. Her voice is silky and good-natured. Respectful, but not overawed. When she hikes in thick brush with her kids, Jeanne says, she has them all trained to "hoot and holler."

"We yell: 'Here comes dinner,'" she laughs.

She talks about how bears are solitary for much of their lives, how zoologists think much aggression is a bluff because the possibility of injury is so high, even for the winners.

"They aren't simple stimulus-response machines," Jeanne says.

The moon-faced man asks if it's true that you only have to be really careful around breeding season. Jeanne shakes her head, her ponytail swinging.

"Aggression is important to bears all their lives," she says. "And not just for males. It helps adult females maintain control over an area for themselves and their offspring."

Jeanne lights the fire in the middle of the circle, produces a big thermos and pours hot cocoa into mugs. Maretta helps hand them around. She wishes the program would last longer.

"Are you all enjoying your campsites?" Jeanne asks. The fire spits and sizzles.

The mother of the three small children nods vigorously.

Should she mention the music, Maretta wonders? Maybe I'll sound like a poor sport, she thinks. But so what?

Jeanne is smiling, waiting for her reply. Maretta balks at the idea of adding an unpleasant chore to Jeanne's workload tonight. "Everything's great," she says.

The air is smoky now; a hazy shroud from hundreds of campfires clings to the tree tops. She hears the rat-rat-rat of a downy woodpecker hunting for insects.

Maretta feels sorry to leave the fire circle, and even sorrier when she turns down the road to her site. Two auxiliary speakers have been added to the ghetto-blaster. They are arranged on opposite sides of the picnic table for maximum acoustical effect.

"Fucking right," she hears a man say.

It's only nine-thirty, an hour and half until Quiet Hours at the campground. Maretta doesn't feel up to confrontation. Her head hurts and her neck muscles feel taut.

She turns and decides to walk along the lakeside loop that Jeanne pointed out this afternoon. A lovely evening stroll, she'd said. But don't leave it too late.

The narrow trail leads along the river, entering into a shrubby area of dogwood, juniper, prickly rose, chokecherry, labrador tea, and willows. A fog rises, created by the chill glacial water meeting the warmer valley air.

The trail becomes more overgrown, but she keeps on. If she doesn't walk off her anger, she's not sure what she'll do. The last time she felt this way was when one of her students, a sullen Greek named Stavros, handed in homework which she knew had been copied from an American manual called *User's Guide to Literacy.*

Maretta had torn the work into tiny pieces, placed them in a plastic bag and wrapped it in a brown envelope, addressed to Stavros. She even got as far as the post office before she'd thrown the parcel in a garbage container.

Now the path is narrowing and she has to push the willows out of her way. She'd turn back, but it's probably shorter just to continue on the loop.

And then she's out in a clearing, crossing over a small bridge to an island. She stops to enjoy the view. The sky has a pearlish cast, and the river shimmers like liquid mercury. A slight wind blows wisps of light brown hair onto her cheek.

When she sees the bear, she doesn't start. It's almost as though she expected it. The bear is on the other side of the river, a huge brown form pawing at the water's edge. Maretta takes in the humped back, the dished-in face, and then two scampering balls of fluff. A mother with two cubs.

"Christ," she thinks, then realizes the wind is to her back. Good. That means the bear probably has Maretta's scent; the worst thing would be to surprise her.

The sow takes no notice of her. She watches in fascination as the two cubs romp between the mother's legs.

The mother puts up with their antics once, twice, three times. Then, the fourth time, she cuffs each of them, solid smacks that send them reeling back on the sand. The cubs scurry back into the woods.

The mother stands erect, sniffing the air. Then she disappears after the cubs.

Maretta hums the chords from "Tea for the Tillerman" as she walks back. She forces herself not to run. Her neck aches.

When she returns to the campsite, she sees with relief that her neighbours have retreated indoors. She hears the thud of bass, but not the lyrics. Occasional squeals of laughter punctuate the darkening mountain night.

Now her knees collapse. She zips open the tent, crawls inside and pulls out the wax earplugs she bought at the IDA on the way out of town. Then she hangs a flashlight from a string in the middle of the tent. Circles of orange light bounce against the red nylon walls.

She pulls off her T-shirt. She wonders if anyone outside could see her. If her neighbours can make out her shadow? Damn them, she thinks. Damn them all to hell. She yanks the pink wax out of her ear and slowly rolls it into one large repulsive-looking prosthetic ball. Then she flings it against the tent wall.

Maretta wakes early, unzips the tent flap and looks up at a hard blue sky. There's a grey haze on the river. Ring-billed gulls wheel above the water. They must have been there last night, she thinks, but she couldn't even hear them.

She'd promised Anna she would check her answering machine this morning, just in case she decides to drive out for the weekend after all. As she walks up to the telephone booth, she sees that the couple at the next site left empty beer cans on the ground. They gleam in the sunlight. The ghetto-blaster is back on the picnic table.

The pay phone is a few minutes down the road, by a picnic shelter. As she approaches it, she stares up at the peak of Mt. Chephren, black and defiant against the sky. She could make it up to the Elysian Meadows by noon, spend the afternoon exploring and sketching. If she stays till Monday afternoon, she thinks, she'd have time to explore both those meadows and Schäffer Pass.

At the pay phone, she listens to the three rings and imagines her apartment: the stripped pine wood and blue gingham, the light pouring in from the mullioned windows, the swaying glass mobiles inset with pressed wood violets. A place of peace and order.

There's one message on the machine from someone trying to sell Maretta a light bulb that would last three years, and another message from Anna. She won't be driving down; she met "a hunk" at a barbecue the night before. Maretta feels relieved.

Then she hears Jacqueline's voice. How did she get her home number, Maretta wonders? And remembers: the time Jacqueline couldn't finish her homework because she was sick. Maretta said she could call her at home for extra help.

"Meez Sonderlink," Jacqueline is saying, in a plangent voice. "I am just calling to see if I could pick up my homework early? Monday afternoon if possible? Tuesday morning the latest. I haff company coming and haff to do my homework early this week. Please and thank you."

Click.

From where Maretta stands she can see down the road to her campsite.

The young woman emerges from the neighbouring site. The woman walks towards the picnic table, switches on the ghetto-blaster and goes back inside the RV. Maretta tightens her grip on the receiver.

The last message is from The Turtle. She hates to disturb Maretta on the weekend, but she has a new student she absolutely has to place right away and could she be a sport and take just one more? And if possible could she pick up her file on Monday, so she's all ready for her on Tuesday?

Maretta starts to place the receiver back on its holder, then looks up at Mt. Chephren and feels a breath of glacial air cut right into her heart.

She keeps her eyes on the peak, because what she is seeing is astonishing: Anna's papers scattered over the highway, Jacqueline with her round blue demanding eyes, the way the woman at the next campsite looked at her as if she were some kind of noxious weed to be pulled out by the roots.

The receiver feels as weighty as a boulder. Maretta holds the coiled metal telephone cord in one hand and the receiver in the other, and pulls. The rubber base that attaches the cord to the receiver stretches, then snaps out with alarming ease. She places the disconnected receiver back on its mount and leaves the metal cord as it is, drooping beside the pay phone like a sleeping snake.

Her heels smack the gravel as she strides to the picnic table beside her campsite.

You say you love me twice as much
While you kick me on the ground.

Without stopping she scoops up the radio in one hand and continues to the river's edge. "There," she shouts to the gulls. The radio flashes silver as it arcs over the water and disappears with a gentle splash.

Going Through the Gooseneck

I FEEL IAN'S EYES ON my back as I dip my paddle into the Athabasca River. We've been squeezed into his two-person German kayak since just after lunch, when we launched downstream from the pulp mill town in northwestern Alberta.

I turn around for a last glimpse of the Rockies, but already they've dissolved into a distant purple wash. The air smells of lodgepole pine and rotten eggs. I return to slicing the glacier-fed river with my paddle.

No doubt Ian has been measuring the kinetic efficiency of my stroke, the amount of effort transmitted through my shoulder muscles and biceps to the paddle. Ultimately, of course, he must be measuring my contribution to the net propulsion of our little voyage.

What does Ian imagine to be the ideal amount of energy suited to my task, I wonder? No need for me to question if I'm living up to that ideal. I know only too well that I am not.

"Make larger whirlpools," Ian says, in that tone that really means: 'See, you're being incompetent again.'"

"I'm trying," I reply.

For Christ's sake, I remind myself of a three-year-old, although I just turned thirty-four. My graduate students, the ones who fight to get into tutorials by Dr. Alyce Redekop, would never believe my verbal tiptoeing.

I flex my arms, then hold the paddle above my head to catch the wind, like a sail. It's late spring; the river is engorged, in flood. The current is so strong that I feel I'm being hurtled along on the back of a gigantic turquoise python. What I do not say is that this must be our last trip together.

Ian Kristoff and I met at a provincial conference on Alberta arts and crafts education in Red Deer. I'd been asked to deliver a paper on the relationship between art and mythology in prehistoric northern cultures, and Ian on his success in encouraging native Indian craftsmen in Alberta to develop and market their wares. The short bio the conference coordinator handed out described Ian as "playing a key role in the development of glassblowing in the Pacific Northwest, raising it to a new level of sophistication and complexity." A friend pointed him out to me; he was tall and had a thatch of pale blond hair and a heavy jaw that I took for a sign of arrogance, before I saw all the wistfulness in his eyes.

That night at the banquet, Ian was seated across the table from me. He arrived late, with profuse apologies. Up close, I could see that he was older than his bio photo showed, in his late thirties at least. He kept brushing a shock of hair from his forehead and shaking his head back, and drawing doodle after doodle on the paper napkins. When the waiter came round to pour drinks, Ian dug two identical glasses out of a case.

"My own," he explained, placing a long cylinder of glass in front of me. It was imbedded with a design of sinuous dark green leaves, like a weed-choked pond.

"See if it works," he said, with a shy smile. "I'm planning to donate them to the native education auction tomorrow."

"What a nice idea," I said, feeling stupid. I didn't know what else to say. I guessed the glasses must be worth at least one hundred dollars a pair. Later I found out that Ian could have sold them for five hundred dollars apiece in Banff or Vancouver, and that he'd already lost his private studio and was having to make do with a commercial one.

During the meal – prime Alberta beef – we discovered a mutual passion for the photography of Ansel Adams, the architecture of Douglas Cardinal, and the nonfiction of Edward Abbey.

"*Desert Solitaire* changed my life," Ian said. "Remember how it opens, the guy saying he's looking at the most beautiful spot in the world, and that there are many such places?"

I nodded. It was a passage I often thought of, driving hour after hour through dark spruce forest, searching for the tellers of folk tales.

Just as the education minister rose to deliver his after-dinner speech,

Ian slipped me a note on a napkin. "I can't take this," he scribbled.

So we excused ourselves. Ian borrowed a snowmobile – which we both pretended to loathe – and we lurched and bounced through the nearby fields for hours under the northern lights, making ourselves dizzy from the joy of it. We even tried to throw snowballs at each other; they fell apart like icing sugar in the cold. I, who had felt middle-aged at nineteen, jammed snow down his chest and his jeans.

The next morning, I found a tiny glassblown paperweight of a polar bear in front of my room at the hotel, with a note: "To Alyce, also fragile, also strong."

That was three years ago. When we got back to Edmonton, Ian just gradually moved into my small house near the university. We got married about a year later. We didn't do it for appearance's sake, of course. I think we just wanted to prove to our friends that we were that committed. Ian bought me a wedding ring of engraved silver. He didn't want to wear a ring himself; he said he had never worn a ring in his life.

After the cutbacks, when Ian lost his teaching job at the community college, he converted my one-car garage into a studio. I cashed in some term deposits to pay for a kiln. I didn't mind moving my home office down to a corner of the living room. Ian needed the extra space upstairs to display his expanding collection of goblets, bowls, perfume bottles, lamp shades, and figurines.

Thunderheads gather behind us by four o'clock, and we make camp early. Set up the dome tent, tether it to the straggly willows, secure the kayak high on the rocky beach.

I cook macaroni, congratulating myself on bringing some extra-sharp shredded cheddar. We eat out of the two cooking pots, gazing at the fast-flowing river and listening to the gulls.

Ian leaves me to scrape out the pots while he does some sketching. "Be sure you don't throw soap in the river," he says.

After I finish the dishes, we walk around the forlorn island. A few patches of scrubby grass struggle for a foothold; a dying poplar stands in the middle. But mostly the island is a heap of brush and rock.

"Want to play a game?" Ian asks.

He draws a circle in the sand with a stick and hands me a smooth pink stone. I aim for the circle, miss, try again, miss again. Ian takes his time selecting exactly the right stone with his long-fingered artist's hands. He aims, goes dead centre. He only wants to play games he can win.

I can't keep putting off this conversation. It's unfair to us both.

Two years ago when we camped on this river, we saw a flash of green late at night. Later we found out that a rather large meteorite had fallen into a lake to the south.

When we got back to the city, Ian actually called up an astronomer at the Space Sciences Centre, and got the whole story. Then he designed his Comet series of blown-glass vessels that won him mention in *Canadian Art* and a feature article in *The Globe and Mail*. Each vessel is composed of bands of bright yellow and green, joined by smoky indigo. The *Globe* writer praised his "whimsy, wit and technical mastery." An oil company purchased the whole Comet series; it's on display at their Calgary head office.

Ian feels that he hasn't had a really original idea since then.

I go back to the camp, find my flashlight, rub on insect repellent. I dig my notebook out of my backpack, to jot down a few thoughts I've had during the day.

The research for my second book is almost finished. I've been collecting folk tales throughout northern Alberta and British Columbia, trying to see how they fit into other patterns of North American spirituality. Already I'm certain this book will be better than I ever hoped. The thought doesn't cheer me.

When I reach for my notebook, I recall that at first, Ian didn't even want me to take research notes on these trips. He said my books would just take up too much space.

Why don't I just tell him?

Ian returns, carrying a huge river-polished rock. He lays it down before me as gently as if it were an ostrich egg. "It's rose quartzite," he says. "Run your fingers over it."

I close my eyes and let my fingers probe the glassy surface. Ian is right, of course. I sense the shape of the rock inside my nerve endings.

"That's the only way you can really see something," Ian says, clenching his jaw in the slightly patronizing way he talks to his students. "It has to be experienced."

I know that I am not the only woman Ian has taken on these trips. Once, when we were just getting to know each other, I went to borrow a pen from his desk, and came across a picture of a woman standing by the kayak, on a shoreline like this one.

"I brought you a bouquet," Ian says. He sticks a wilted purple aster behind my ear.

I have known that I will leave Ian since February 2 at 10:30 p.m. That was the moment I discovered that one of Ian's students had inadvertently destroyed all my notes on Josie Crow.

I met Josie up at Fort Simpson in the Northwest Territories, at the time the Pope was supposed to visit. She must have been about ninety years old, although no one knew for sure. She knew variations on the old Napi legends that had never before been documented, but she wouldn't let me use a tape recorder. She said plain words were better. About a month after I spoke with Josie, she died.

I'd been preparing a lecture that night in February, and had to go back to campus, so Ian invited his class into the house after a studio session. It was cold, and we'd run out of kindling. And there were all my notes, on cheap yellow paper, just lying about, because I was just starting to transcribe them. I should have had them Xeroxed right away, but I was still disorganized from having to move my office and thought they'd be okay there for a few days.

Later, when I asked Ian why he hadn't done anything, he claimed not to know what all the fuss was about. He insisted that I must have internalized Josie's words, the way he carries the concept of an arresting shape in his head.

"You want me to fail," I yelled.

Oh, he apologized all right. Even offered to find out if he could transfer some of his frequent flyer points to my name, so we could fly to San Francisco for Valentine's Day. He didn't know that in a way, I'd already taken flight.

When I wake up, a grey mist is rising from the river. I hear rain pattering down the fly of the tent. We eat inside: instant porridge, dried fruit, peanut butter and bread, powdered orange juice, instant coffee.

Today we will go through Gooseneck Rapids, the only really dangerous part of the trip. We tie down all our supplies, snugly snap on the kayak skirt, zip the camera into a waterproof bag.

At the last moment, Ian heaves the quartzite rock into the bow. He says he wants to use it as inspiration for a nonfunctional lamp of clear-cut cast glass. "Isn't that going to weigh us down too much?" I ask.

"We'll be all right," Ian says. His jaw is clenched.

The current moves along faster than ever on this section of the river. We work to stay in the deepest part, gliding along under the steep Pre-Cambrian cliffs.

We start into the throat of the rapids. I've studied these waters in the *Athabasca River Reach Reports:* they actually do twist in the shape of a gooseneck. We hug the right shore, staying just beyond the clutch of the heaving rapids in the centre. In minutes we clear the first curve of the gooseneck.

So far, so good. Just one more bend to go. Then it happens. The bow heaves under high rollers that twist into an eddy. I grip the paddle tightly and lower my head.

"Draw!" Ian yells. "Draw!"

I obey with more strength than I knew I had. And then, three-quarters of the way through, I see a shining black rock straight ahead. It's too late to turn, but the rock is almost completely submerged. If we're lucky we'll just scrape the keel.

A second later, the bow smashes into the rock. That damned quartzite. The kayak spins round, broadside to the current. Ian can't hold the kayak straight by himself. We're capsizing. I'm sideways, now I'm underwater, swirling, grabbing for the kayak.

I seem to sink forever. Then I surface with a jolt. I grab for the cloth holds on the kayak's stern.

I see an orange blob to the side. It's Ian, headed into the centre of the eddy. He seems unconscious. I reach out my free arm to grab him. But then I pull back. For an instant. An instant where unspeakable possibilities run through my mind.

I feel a thrill of terror that has nothing to do with the river.

My arm brushes against Ian's. I grab his hand. Is he dragging me off the boat? I hold on as tightly as I can to both his hand and the kayak, and do my best to angle our way to shore. Ian's eyes are open, but he doesn't say anything. In what seems like five minutes, but is probably five seconds, I feel the water-polished river bottom under my feet.

Ian collapses on the rocky beach. He has a bruise on his forehead that's turning purple. I pull out the first-aid kit from my pack and apply an antibiotic and a cold pack. Miracle of miracles, inside the layers of green garbage bags, I find dry clothing. We count our losses: one paddle, one water container we can live without, the quartzite, a few bottles of Coke, and maybe one mild concussion.

"Not your fault," Ian says.

I build a fire and crouch further into its warmth. As I look through the flames, I see the river waiting. The river has carried me to a place where I can finally summon the strength to end my silence.

Erratics

Half an hour after they ski away from the parking lot, a mechanized whine slices the mild February air.

Kathleen Edwards-Mattison turns to her husband, Tim Mattison, but his fortyish choir boy's face is expressionless. Bright yellow wires descend from under his ear muffs; no doubt he is lost in Mozart piano concertos. She steps off the track with one ski and lets him glide by, his crimson fleece jacket bright as a geranium against the snowy hills and the sky of white bone.

The sound seems further away now but she needs a moment to regain her easy diagonal stride. Something pulls in her stomach, the way it did this morning when she tangled silk yarn on a simple running stitch for the National Wilderness Society quilt. Were the knots trying to tell her something, she wondered?

"You haven't actually got the commission yet, have you?" Tim had asked at breakfast.

Kathleen decided not to mention that Grant O'Gara from the wilderness society had called on Tuesday to query the price she'd quoted.

"It's all hand-stitched, of course," she'd said. As if he didn't know.

"You'll be pricing yourself out of our reach," Grant replied. Voice lukewarm, like thermos tea. "One of these days we'll have to stoop to something machine-made."

Of course he was joking.

Her face is hot; a film of light sweat seeps down her back. She pulls off her toque and stuffs it into a side pocket, then removes a brochure from the provincial recreation department called *Winter Fun.*

They should reach the Spruce View Trail in about half an hour, according to the map. "This thirteen-kilometre route around Kettle Lake is the longest and most scenic ski trail in the reserve," Kathleen reads.

Crude contour lines illustrate how the new recreational reserve, in the moraine country of northeastern Alberta, forms part of a broad plateau rising sixty metres or so above the surrounding prairie. "A landscape of rolling hills, aspen forests, hay meadows, sloughs and hillocks," says the brochure. Kathleen has heard the area referred to as uplands, and that's how she likes to think of it. There's something cheering and jaunty about the term, she thinks, although Tim says it's stretching the point.

When he called from the office this morning to say a client had postponed the afternoon seminars, she'd actually tapped her needle against the telephone receiver in her studio.

"Perfect timing," she'd said. "We'll have a glorious ski. Plus I could really use one more look at Kettle Lake." She'd chosen the lake as the model for the appliqué centrepiece on the wilderness quilt.

"You must already have a million photos," Tim had teased.

"They're not the same as my own eyes."

Kathleen knows she should push on, but now she wants to take in the pale mottled sky, the reddish tangle of willows, the surface of the snow-banks laced by footprints of voles and other small animals. The early afternoon light is diffuse, a soft creamy glow that seems to leap from the earth as much as the sky.

She imagines her brain cells storing these images. Senses a tingle in her fingers at the thought of translating them into fabric blocks and squares and circles: the tree trunks of sepia sailcloth, sky of ice-blue silk, perhaps a layer of white voile over dark grey for the snow. Connecting them all with her palette of stitches: herringbone, feather, buttonhole, satin, whipping. Sprinkling in coral knots for snowflakes.

"You know, the images I rely on never come to me on command," she told her friend Dorothy, a fellow fibre artist, when they met in Strathcona for cappuccino last week. "They only come when I relax. Outdoors, usually."

"Lucky you," said Dorothy. "Mine usually come from nightmares. I keep a notebook on my bedside table and write them down as soon as I wake up."

"Nightmares are about the last thing I want to remember," Kathleen said.

"What if all the places we relax in disappear, little by little?" she had asked Tim on the drive out. She'd just finished reading a newspaper article about an MLA who wanted freer access for all-terrain vehicles in provincial park and wilderness areas.

"You worry too much," Tim replied in his city planner's voice, thin, methodical as paper clips. "The guy's just floating a balloon."

Ahead of them on the highway the flashing red lights of a police cruiser came into view. Tim slowed down, then came to a stop behind the police car. A late model sports car straddled the centre line, the metal of its hood so smashed and wrinkled it might have been foil. The driver of a tow truck was trying to attach a hook under the front of the car. Kathleen could see wavering tire tracks in the ditch ahead. A rusty pickup truck sat in the middle of the ditch, upright and seemingly undamaged.

The police officer walked over to Tim.

"Just be a few minutes," he said.

"Anyone hurt?" Tim asked.

"Just a few scratches."

Tim pulled his laptop from his briefcase and started balancing his computerized chequebook. Kathleen's hands fluttered in her lap. "We could lose twenty minutes of light because of this guy," she said. She imagined sticking a giant quilting needle into the roof of the damaged sports car and hurling it into the air, leaving the highway clear and uncluttered. Could almost hear the rip of the metal, the smell of oil.

"Actually," said Tim, "this sort of thing could probably be avoided if headlights were required during the day. Like in Sweden. Maybe I'll write a letter to the editor or something."

She suspected Tim actually would have written a letter then and there, but the policeman waved them by.

Kathleen catches up to Tim on the flats part way between the parking lot and Kettle Lake. "Can you take off your Walkman for a minute?" she shouts.

Tim tucks the earplugs into a breast pocket. The high-pitched buzzing noise is distant but persistent. "So that's what's bugging you," he says. "It's a long way off, you know. Probably not even in the reserve. Even then...."

Kathleen can guess what he's thinking. The trails in the Kettle Lake area of the reserve were only closed to motorized traffic last fall. You couldn't expect instant compliance.

"My advice?" he says. "Ignore it."

He inserts the earphones again and disappears down the next hill. The hickory laminate of his Finnish wooden skis shines, making them look like brown arrows: a Christmas present to him from Kathleen.

"You realize if you break or damage a tip we can't replace it," the clerk at the outdoor store said when Kathleen placed the special order. "Everything's gone fibreglass. There isn't much demand for wooden skis anymore."

What Kathleen hears next from Tim is a shout. Not a fear shout. An adrenalin shout. A kid's shout, a Holy Cow Jumping Jesus Whoopee-do-is-this-ever-fun kind of shout.

The buzzing sound has stopped. An ease and lightness ripples through her body. Kathleen starts to double-pole down the hill, then decides just to glide. You never knew what could be around these corners. Coming around a turn, a skier could be surprised to find, close enough to touch, a mound of snow-covered granite the height of a human being. Erratics, the brochure calls them, deposited thousands of years ago by immense sheets of glacial ice. They make her uneasy, the way they appear when she least expects them; she thinks of them as deviants, runaways from another wilder, harsher age.

The wind stings her cheeks, cold and exhilarating. She feels her heart pumping. This is what I'm here for, she thinks. She resumes double-polling. To hell with the erratics. Her skis are sleek wooden needles speeding across a blanket of white wool.

Tim waits beside a wooden bridge over a frozen creek. Kathleen is glad she convinced him to exchange his wire-rim glasses for new ones with coronation red frames. They give him a buoyant, reckless look she likes.

"This is absolutely superb," Tim says. His voice louder than it needs to be because of the Walkman. "They must have just groomed the track this morning. We really couldn't have scheduled this any better."

That sound again, much closer. Kathleen looks back. Two machines are speeding towards them. Against the chalky landscape, the gleaming black metal reminds her of the carapaces of giant black beetles.

"Jesus," she says.

"They may simply not be aware of the regulations here," Tim says. His cheeks are deeply flushed; with his high brow and fine blond hair, he still reminds Kathleen of a young tenor in an Anglican choir.

The snowmobiles approach, side by side. One is a big black Arctic Cat EXP, the driver a white-haired man who appears to be in his late fifties, the other a small Yamaha, driven by a woman, slightly younger-looking, with frizzy brown hair and a pleasant, somewhat tentative smile. The two wear sheepskin gloves and matching snowmobile suits of practical navy nylon. A mass of yellow bungee cords anchors leather saddlebags to the back of the machines; Kathleen has the fleeting impression of iron freighters churning across an ocean of snow.

"Grand day," the man calls over the machine's shudder.

He raises his visor, revealing a thin, sunburned face, seamed skin pulled tight across his skull. A smile that's service-club polite.

Kathleen nods. She is about to explain that motorized vehicles are no longer allowed in this part of the reserve when he pulls something out of his pocket.

"This yours?" He holds out her toque, the Icelandic wool one Dorothy knitted for Kathleen last Christmas. She loves the soft greys, the exuberant bursts of snowflakes.

"Yes, thank you so much."

She again starts to say something about the area being closed to snowmobiles, but the man is revving up his machine and easing by her. Tim puts up his hand and steps in front of the machine.

"This is actually for cross-country skiers only," he says. He has to shout above the machine but sounds polite anyway.

"Aw, c'mon," the man says.

"We're not saying you can't skidoo around here," says Tim. "We just wondered if you could leave these ski tracks intact for us? There's another part of the reserve open for snowmobiles."

The man smiles and shakes his head. "I've been skidooing out here for twenty years," he says, his voice steady. "We're not doing any harm."

He waves to his wife, who has a dazed look on her face. Then he accelerates around Tim. The snowmobiles vanish down the track.

Kathleen scrunches the toque into a tight ball with her fist and squeezes it into her day pack. Gas fumes hang in the air. The ski tracks have disappeared, the snow pressed and churned and flattened into icy ridges by the machines' treads.

Tim shrugs, reinserts the earphones and starts to ski along the tread marks. Kathleen attempts to follow, but she can't get the grip she needs for a decent kick and glide. The skis slide all over. She moves across to the unpacked snow on the side, but sinks up to mid-calf.

She pushes a willow branch away from her face. Ugly, scrubby thing.

"If those snowmobilers go on the Spruce View Trail once they reach the lake, they'll spoil our whole afternoon," she calls out to Tim. "I'd like to attach them permanently to those machines."

She allows herself to imagine binding the snowmobile couple with a giant needle threaded with thick cord. Securing them to an erratic in some forlorn part of the reserve. A nice whipping stitch would do it, something fast and secure. Leaving them for another Ice Age.

She remembers that Tim can't hear her anyway with the Walkman in his ear. No doubt he'd say it was too early to expect the worst. If they're lucky, the snowmobilers will head out across the lake and disappear into the section of the reserve where snowmobiling is permitted.

They climb a small rise where another cross-country ski trail, Running Dog, veers to the right. Kathleen remembers it as being shorter and less scenic than Spruce View.

"Maybe we should opt for Running Dog today," Tim says. He removes one of the earplugs. "Spare ourselves a lot of aggravation."

"And let them win?"

"We can't exactly physically stop them. Besides…" he pulls a notebook out of his pocket. "I've got their licence plate numbers. They'll either be fined or at least get a warning."

"I was really counting on Spruce View," Kathleen says.

Back in November Kathleen had watched in the basement of their house in Edmonton as Tim spread tar on the bases of their skis. Then he lit a propane torch and warmed the viscous black liquid till it bubbled. She felt a tang in her nostrils.

They left the tar on for a few minutes, then rubbed it down with hard, even strokes. "Get it right into the base," Tim said. "That's what gives it strength." People could use some kind of base, Kathleen thought. Something to protect their nerves from the bruises and scratches of everyday life.

When they finished, she ran her fingers over the bases again and again. They were as smooth as the heartwood of young poplar. That sensation formed the basis of Kathleen's proposal to the wilderness society; she's depending on the commission to finance her experimental work. She envisioned a series of appliquéd blocks, each a close-up of the trunk of a northern hardwood. The blocks will frame fluffy cotton puffs or stretched white silk in the shape of Kettle Lake, rimmed with spruce.

In the proposal, she promised a work that would be "a robust, cheerful tribute to the restorative power of the Canadian wilderness." She is no Mildred Guthrie, Kathleen often tells Dorothy, that American fibre artist who actually stitched up a "Watergate Quilt." She's no Irene Preston, either, that other woman Dorothy so admires, who caused such a sensation with her Hudson River quilt in the sixties. All that pollution and neglect depicted in broadcloth.

"You call that art?" she'd asked Dorothy. "I call it fibre graffiti."

Dorothy teases Kathleen that her work is "unrelentingly uplifting." Kathleen likes to joke back that she's after "sailcoth sonnets, linen lyrics." When she won second prize in the Great Quilters of Canada contest last year, sponsored by *Canadian Life*, the adjudicator wrote that her designs "are especially captivating; alive with a delightful sense of whimsy. No shadows ever seem to taint the pictorial appliqué of Kathleen Edwards-Mattison."

"Don't you ever feel like working on something absolutely sordid?" Dorothy teased, when she told her about the proposal for the hardwood series.

"No," she said. "Why should I?"

"Just wondering."

Dorothy herself has just finished a collage featuring five hundred patchwork pieces, shaped to resemble cruise missiles. The missiles are flying over a quilt the shape of Alberta.

"Those snowmobilers are probably just headed for the lake," says Tim. "We'll likely only have a few more minutes of this to go through. Just the roller coaster section."

Usually Kathleen looks forward to the series of short sharp hills running down to the lake. Today she feels uneasy.

"You first," she says.

The wind is in her face. In the distance she sees Kettle Lake, and what appear to be two dark dots moving across the ice. She's too far away to identify them. The western sky is darkening, a gray flannel sheet unfolding to the horizon.

Tim speeds over the first bumpy hill and Kathleen waits for his whoops of joy, but instead hears only the twittering of chickadees flitting in the aspen branches, tiny black bibs trembling. Tim's favorite bird; he admires their sense of decorum. They usually take their turn at the feeder, he says. Not like the purple finches Kathleen prefers, so pretty and so bossy, driving all the other birds away.

Then she hears a yell.

She starts down. A big crude snowplow is what's called for here, something she knows she can control.

She finds Tim in a crumple, halfway down the slope.

"Cripes," he says. He is on his stomach, head toward the bottom of the hill, face and hair covered with snow, his arms and legs splayed. One of the lenses in his new glasses is missing.

"What happened?" Kathleen asks.

"I don't know. I heard a crunch and my skis just went out from under me."

He gets up slowly. A breeze shakes the branches above them and releases woolly puffs of snow.

Kathleen makes a feeble attempt to find the missing lens but they both know it's useless. Nearby the treads of the machines have exposed the tip of a rock.

"Look," she calls out.

"Son-of-a-bitch," says Tim.

He rustles through his pack. Stubby cylinders of green wax, blue wax, orange wax, special white wax, a cork and a scraper spill out on the snow. He finds a small roll of duct tape and wraps it around the cracked frame, then puts on the glasses.

"I can't stand this," he says after a moment. "The vision in one eye is normal and everything's fuzzy in the other. I'm going to get a jim-dandy headache."

"Give them to me. And the tape."

Kathleen tears a small piece of cardboard from a Kleenex pack, shapes it to fit the missing lens and tapes it on.

"Thanks." Tim pats his breast pocket. "I've still got that notebook."

They execute basic christies to the bottom of the roller coaster section, which meets the shore of Kettle Lake. Tim skis up to the wooden map at the beginning of the Spruce View Trail.

"The track's good," he says.

Kathleen senses a loosening in her diaphragm. Already she doesn't want the Spruce View Trail to end. She sees herself floating on white froth, her vexations ironed away by the gliding movements and the cool, intoxicating air.

The grind of engines startles them both. Kathleen turns to see the Arctic Cat easing up to a cedar shelter a few metres back from the lake.

"Well, let's get going, shall we?" Tim says. Cold sunlight glints for a minute and she notices what appears to be a fine crack in the laminate of his right ski.

"Just a minute," she calls, but Tim is already several strides ahead.

The trail above Kettle Lake is so narrow that alder and willow branches push against her shoulders on either side. Through the trees Kathleen looks down at the lake. Its surface is no bowl of cotton puffs, no stretched sheet of white silk. Skidoo marks zigzag across the snow, mashing it here, exposing blue ice there. The sight reminds Kathleen of the remains of a wintry demolition derby.

Tim is already around the next corner.

From somewhere behind, the sound of an engine.

And then Kathleen is reaching for a hefty branch on a dead aspen tree beside the trail. She twists and breaks it off, hearing the sound of trucks, the hum of sewing machines and pocketbook computers, Grant's careful voice; seeing Dorothy's quilted cruise missiles, splattered oil, crushed twigs. The images seem to spin around her, faster and faster, so that for a moment she's not certain which direction is up and which is down. For a few seconds she is conscious only of sheer whiteness divided into tiny blinking squares, then transformed into black squares. The squares are shrinking and shriveling and splitting, like the sections of she saw on a topographical map of Alberta and British Columbia, with logging roads and all-terrain vehicle trails and grazing pastures and seismic lines scissoring across here, snipping away there.

The next minute she's placing the branch across the trail, supporting it on top of the thick waist-high shrubbery on either side. The shrubbery sags a bit, but holds the weight.

That'll give them the message.

Or should she lower the branch a bit? How high is the seat on a snowmobile, anyway? She's never driven or ridden on one.

Oh well. The section of trail here is fairly flat. Besides, the branch isn't much thicker than her wrist. It would snap if anyone drove or skied into it. Likely it will fall down in a minute, anyway.

The vision of yellow bungee cords springs into her head, like those on the back of the snowmobiles. One of them would have been better.

She strides away, polling hard. The only sounds are the slipping of the skis against the snow and her own breathing, gasping and irregular, then deeper and more rhythmic.

The tracks on the Spruce View Trail are fast and even. Kathleen doesn't speak to Tim, but she hears his reassuring whoops ahead. On the long rolling hills she has the impression of being unfettered by gravity, carried by wooden wings along a ridge of clouds.

The light is failing by the time they approach the parking lot; the sky has started to turn shades of deep mauve, violet and coral.

One snowmobile – it looks like the smaller one they saw on the trail – is parked at an odd angle in the middle of the lot. A man stands beside the machine and looks up as they approach. He is of medium height and wears a khaki parka. A provincial ranger's badge is stitched onto his breast pocket.

Tim and Kathleen snap off their skis.

The ranger says hello, then looks at them closely.

"You on the Spruce View Trail this afternoon?"

Tim nods.

"See anything unusual?"

"No. Why?"

"Had to ask. A couple was along there this afternoon; the guy fell off his snowmobile. Must have been going too fast, because he took a bad spill. Got a twig in one eye, poor bugger. Then he went into shock so bad he can't even speak. Looks to me like he's probably going to lose that eye. It took his wife an hour to get him back here."

"That's terrible," says Kathleen. She feels a lightness in her head. Thank goodness for the ski poles to steady her.

"The woman says she thought her husband swerved into the bushes to avoid some kind of obstacle. Says it was on the Spruce View Trail, just on the other side of the lake. You wouldn't happen to know anything about it, would you?"

"No," says Tim. "We were on that trail this afternoon, but we didn't see anything out of the ordinary."

The ranger looks straight at Tim for a moment, then shrugs.

"Yeah, well," he says. "Had to ask. I found a broken branch there. Cross-country skiers have been known to do that sort of thing once in a while. Don't know why anyone would bother swerving into the bushes to avoid it, though. Of course, he'd had a bit to drink. And he shouldn't have been going so fast anyway. Matter of fact, he shouldn't have been on that trail."

Kathleen leaves Tim talking to the ranger and walks toward the car, where she fits her skis onto the roof rack. What happens to your peripheral vision when you only have one eye, she wonders? Does the world appear narrower? Flat? She shakes her head. An erratic thought.

They drive home in silence. The city is backdropped by a winter sunset of hazy blues and salmon pinks. Even the gas processing plant by Sherwood Park appears sprightly in this light, although she usually considers it a blemish on the landscape.

They Don't Make Lakefront Anymore

We are cleaning out the cabin. It's February, and so cold even the ice fishermen have departed. The tenants used up all the oil before they went back to Ontario, so the furnace is useless. I built a fire out of necessity, instead of the usual anticipation of pleasure. We wear down parkas over thick cords and polypropylene long johns, Gord and I as we sort out what we'll keep and what we'll sell.

I'm on the back porch, emptying glass jars into the trash, when I come across the red aluminum casserole. I take off the lid, the one with the plastic stay-cool knob I melted in the oven years ago, and look down on the frozen brown remains. A few carrots, still bright orange, stick out from the white blobs of fat and congealed sea of gravy. Is this the dinner Dianne was preparing for that last night?

I stare at this pathetic stew, and I see for the first time how events entrapped us all. I can even see Everett and Eva again, walking across the ice.

We placed the ad in *The Edmonton Journal* in October, 1981, eighteen months after we had bought the cabin. A Friday. I remember clearly because it was one day after the Bank of Canada raised interest rates again, and at that time the bank rate was always set on Thursdays.

Everett Prociuk was the second person to call. Just in from Ontario, too dumb to know the bloom was already off the boom. He had a job lined up at the vinyl chloride plant at Fort Saskatchewan, inspecting pipes. He had a wife, Dianne, and a four-year-old kid, Eva.

He was – what? – twenty-four, twenty-five. I never asked. I can see the three of them, standing by the lakeshore in front of the cabin where we met them on a Saturday afternoon. Everett was blond and stocky, with slanted shoulders. He wore what Gord called "the typical drifter outfit" – blue jeans, lined blue jean jacket, a peaked Husky Oil cap. I can't remember much more. I guess I never really looked at him.

Dianne I have an even harder time seeing. Maybe that's because her memory makes me feel more guilty. She wore a grown-out red Afro, and one of those high school jackets that I can never understand grown women wearing, one with her name emblazoned on the sleeve. I doubt if she was twenty-one. She had a lazy left eye. Even then I never wanted to look directly at her.

The little girl, Eva, clasped her father's hand. She had grey eyes that reminded me of startled question marks, and thick brown hair, chin length, which would have been pretty if it hadn't been so dull. Her skin was marble-white; purple veins stood out on her eyelids when she blinked.

Eva didn't care about the cabin. All she could see was the lake. "Boat ride, daddy, boat ride," she kept saying.

I was worried right away when I saw the child. The cabin wasn't really winterized, just set above the ground on concrete blocks. The floor stayed cold no matter how high we turned up the furnace. Give me credit for this. I did warn them.

"We can add some insulation, if you don't mind paying for the materials," Everett said.

Naturally Gord and I agreed. Lack of maintenance or physical deterioration of any kind bothers my husband, although not enough to bring him to action. For example, he'd been meaning for ages to install that antique stained glass window in the study of the cabin, the one he inherited from his aunt in Montreal and that caused us so much trouble. The window was hexagonal, composed of hundreds of tiny cast-glass hexagons in shades of deep rose, china blue and purple. When you placed your eyes close to the hexagons it was like peering through a kaleidoscope, the world whirled with sharp, six-angled figures. The colours of a winter sunrise and sunset seemed to be encased within a thousand glistening ice crystals.

Gord kept that window wrapped away in a trunk in the study, thinking some day he'd get around to installing it, but I never bet on that happening any time soon. When he was a teen-ager, he never even built brick-and-board shelves. "My parents would just hire someone to do the job," he said.

Gord grew up in Ottawa and came out here in the seventies. Like most easterners, he thought of Alberta as jobs and money. He's a salesman for a company that manufactures technical equipment for the oil and gas industry. He spends every other week in the West Pembina oil field, living out of a motel in Drayton Valley, although all that might change now if the layoffs continue.

What Gord really likes to do, though, is to hunch over his beloved maps. Mistakes infuriate him. He says Alberta appears to have been mapped by blind men with no feeling for the terrain. One map actually showed the Athabasca River instead of the North Saskatchewan flowing through Edmonton.

Gord dreams of producing the definitive atlas of Alberta, which is pretty ambitious considering that you could tuck all England and Scotland into the province, and still have territory left over. I tease him that his fantasy life is filled with meridians. He says mine is filled with words. Both keep us from dwelling too much on our actions.

The Prociuks signed a rental agreement right away. Gord studied every word on the contract before we signed but after that he didn't look at it again. "I hope we haven't made a big mistake," he kept saying.

It was different for me. Back in Edmonton that night, I pulled the document out of the filing cabinet half a dozen times. I couldn't help gazing at our names, Antonia and Gordon Matlock, on the line designated for the landlord. Never before had my signature appeared on that line. Seeing it there made me view myself in a somewhat different way, although I couldn't precisely define what the change was. All I knew for certain was that I felt a little better off than I had before we became landlords.

When was the first time I sensed a coolness between Gord and the Prociuks? Was it that day in early November, when we drove out to the lake and Everett said he'd renovated his uncle's house in Port Credit, and was a little bit of a handyman? Gord replied, in a patronizing sort of way: "Then you should feel at home. That's what we've got out here, all right, a handyman's special."

Gord had gestured to the cabin next door. The owner, a Red Deer high school teacher, had added a cedar porch only last year. Already the porch slanted slightly and the wood had lost its golden sheen because it hadn't been varnished properly. As for the cedar shingle exterior, it never had looked anything but makeshift.

"Peel away those shingles and you'd be looking at a tin ATCO trailer," Gord said. "Aesthetic, eh?"

Before we had finalized our agreement to purchase the cabin the year before, Gord checked to make sure that the bylaws of the summer village wouldn't allow any more trailers to be hauled onto lots and used as permanent housing.

"Gotta start somewhere, though," Everett said. He told us he just loved living beside the lake, away from the noise and crowding of the city. He'd been checking out some of the back lots for sale, he said.

"In a year or two you might lose your renters," he joked. "Depending on how long it takes me to get together a down payment."

Dianne said sunsets were her favorite time. "On a cloudy day, the sky and the lake look like one great big blue cavern," she said.

Gord and I had been tenants during the boom in Edmonton. We'd find a nice suite in an old house, buy a new rug for the living room and a Busy Lizzie for the window. Meanwhile the dark forces of prosperity circled. In would come the *Notice to Vacate*, and we'd be pitched out on the street in thirty days, looking for another house to rent. And then the same thing would happen, unless we settled for a high-rise or a boring suite in a walkup.

Our last landlady, Isabel Abu, was a fat old Iranian matron with a rubbery face. She ran a boutique "for mature figures" in one of those brick malls Edmonton is crawling with. "Don't worry, we're not selling," she said every month when she came to collect the rent.

Back then, landlords could turf you out of a building with only a month's notice. So naturally Isabel Abu delivered our *Notice to Vacate* the day after she'd again reassured us. We found out the house was going to be torn down and a walkup built on the site.

At the same time Isabel gave us notice, she actually had the nerve to offer us another one of her rented houses. She was probably dickering with a developer even as she spoke, the old witch.

Three moves in two years were enough. So we bought our own house, a renovated three-bedroom bungalow in Strathcona. It wasn't large enough for Gord to have a study; we both had to make do with converted bedrooms for home office space. None of the windows was the right size for the stained glass window, which disappointed Gord. He didn't want to just hang it against an existing window, or use it as a wall hanging. "It deserves to be used as it was intended to be used," he insisted.

What we really wanted to do, we decided, was to live in the country.

One day we'd find a place big enough to house one thousand books, a piano, a jacuzzi, Gord's map collection, the antique window. Hence the cabin.

Somehow Gord and I managed to convince ourselves that renting out the cabin worked as well for the Prociuks as it did for us. We didn't want much rent, just enough to take the sting out of the mortgage payments. Sure, they would face a seventy-kilometre commute. So what? With the city vacancy rate at two per cent, they were smart enough to know that if they hadn't lucked onto our cabin, they'd be spending the winter in some godforsaken two-bedroom condo in Mill Woods. Instead, they had an unimpeded view of the ice and lake and northern sky.

"I forgot to warn the Prociuks about the ice fishermen," I said to Gord the night after the November visit.

We saw the cabin for the first time on one of those golden, windless September days. The very best time in Alberta. The lake was Wedgwood blue; the white sails of a marooned catamaran hung limply on the horizon.

The crazy thing is, the cabin was a lot bigger than our house. And it cost almost as much – we could never have made the down payment if Gord's parents hadn't helped out. It stretched clear across the lakefront lot, a rambling, log-cabin affair, with two Rundle rock fireplaces, one in the living room and one in the study, an old-fashioned veranda and three bedrooms, one with double bunks.

The owner, a widowed law professor at the University of Alberta, was retiring and moving out to Victoria. He told us that the cabin – which he called "Timbers" – had been in his family for forty years. He hated to sell, but none of his nieces and nephews could afford it.

When the real estate agent showed us the room he called "the library," Gord nodded at me and I nodded back. Two leaded windows on the south wall looked onto the lake; oak bookshelves lined two walls. The wainscoting needed to be replaced and there were some cracks in the plaster, but the wood mosaic tiles on the floor were sound. Right away Gord could visualize his maps of David Thompson's navigations displayed on the cream ivory wall, along with prints of Wilson's delicate watercolours of the Scott Expedition, and the *Times Atlas of the World* permanently open on a coffee table. I had my own vision: my leather-bound *Nicholas Nickleby* on the gleaming shelves, and the 1898 collector's edition of Joseph Jacob's superbly edited *English Fairy Tales*, with many more stories about trolls and dwarfs than fairies.

"This is the kind of study you see back east," Gord said. Which is one of the highest accolades a room can get from Gord. He says Western Canadians rarely align buildings to take advantage of the light and the landscape.

"You know what would make this room perfect?" he continued. "The antique window on the west wall. It'd be like a permanent sunset."

I was as drawn in by it all as Gord. I could see us sailing the Laser on endless spring days, or sprawled in front of the fireplace on January evenings, reading Thoreau, Barry Lopez, Bruce Chatwin, John McPhee, Edward Abbey. We would leave the city, and I'd freelance. Gord would set up the consulting business for the oil patch he'd been talking about for years.

We made an offer on the cabin that day. It seemed a natural enough thing to do during those boom years. Journalists were always coming out from Ontario – usually from Toronto's national newspaper – and writing envious little squibs about the gold bath taps in Edmonton and Calgary, although I'd never myself seen one. A person couldn't go wrong with real estate, everyone said. Especially lake property. "They don't make lakefront anymore," the real estate agent told us.

Later, when our variable interest payments went up from seven hundred dollars a month to nine hundred, and then to one thousand dollars, Gord and I still weren't worried. Then one day I sat down with a pencil and added up our monthly expenses and our net income, and realized how much it would help to rent the cabin out for the winter. Even then we thought we were facing a temporary problem.

At first everything went smoothly. The Prociuks paid their rent on time, and installed extra insulation. In mid-December, the temperature dipped to minus forty for four days. A few days later, Dianne and Eva stopped off at our house in the city to pick up some more batts of insulation Gord had found in the garage. Dianne had a slight cough but said she was getting over it.

I'd just finished decorating the Christmas tree with silver icicles and had splurged on two sets of miniature blue lights. The icicles refracted the blue light into thousands of shimmering rays. Eva peered at the tree from the entrance.

"Would you like a closer look?" I asked.

"Yes, please," she said. She wouldn't look up at me, just stared straight ahead at my wool skirt and followed me into the living room with careful steps.

After a minute she asked if she could touch one of the decorations.

"Of course," I said. "Why don't I give you one? You can put it on your tree."

"I'll have to ask."

"Oh, I'm sure it will be all right," I said.

I looked at Dianne. She pursed her lips and nodded.

"Thanks," Eva said. She cupped the icicle in her hand and looked me in the eyes for the first time. "This is just like the icicles on our roof," she said.

I got my jacket and led Dianne and Eva into the attached garage where Gord had stacked four thick Fibreglas Pinks against one wall. They were R-35s, just what Everett wanted.

"Like some help?" I asked.

"No, no," Dianne said. "They're light as feathers. Besides, you don't want to have to put your boots on just for this."

I pressed the button on the automatic door opener. The metal runners squealed and suddenly the black night gaped in front of us. Dianne carried the four batts at once, two under each arm. There was something brave about the way she carried those batts, I thought, something fine and unyielding.

I had been with Henday House for four years. Henday was into Canadiana in a big way, and that winter I was responsible for the Alberta section of the new Canadian almanac. Along with one assistant, just out of community college, I was trying to put together contributions from five hundred Albertans, four hundred and eighty of whom wouldn't know what to do with a semicolon if they were clobbered over the head with one. So I was supervising that, trying to polish pithy forty- to one-hundred-word items that somehow encapsulated the spirit of the province. Almanac item: *Alberta's economy has followed a pattern of primary resource exploitation and dependence on external markets, with prices and revenues largely determined by outside economic and political forces.*

Even as I closed the garage door on that December night, I mentally reviewed that section: *Since 1947, the petroleum industry has brought prosperity to both the public and private sectors.*

The first indisputable indication I had that anything was wrong came in early January, when the rental cheque from the Prociuks failed to arrive in the mail. I was at my desk, editing a section on how Alberta has more than one hundred thousand kilometres of pipelines, when Dianne called from work.

"Could we put off paying the rent for a couple of weeks?" she asked. "Eva's had the flu, and I've had to miss some work."

I said sure. I was somewhat annoyed, but not worried. When I told Gord that night, though, he said: what did I expect from drifters, anyway?

Gord is of the opinion that anyone who came out west just for the jobs should be well-prepared. He has no patience for most of the guys on the crews, the useless ones just in from the Maritimes, or Sudbury, dreaming of squeezing a bundle out of Alberta and then getting back east as soon as they can.

"But aren't we all really newcomers?" I asked. Ironically, of course, because I'm a third-generation Albertan. My great-grandparents came out to Strathcona from Germany in the 1890s. Almanac item: *The population of Alberta is characterized by a diverse ethnic heritage. The major ethnic groups are British, German, Ukrainian and Scandinavian. The greatest wave of immigration drew thousands of settlers from northern, central and....*

I'll be the first to admit that I was a little distracted in January. If I hadn't been, maybe things would have turned out differently.

The day after Dianne called, we had a sudden thaw following a week of heavy snowfall. I woke up to find water dripping on the bottom of my bed. The drips were small but regular. After an hour I collected half a pail. All the rental income from the cabin that fall went to pay the roofers.

For Christmas Gord's parents had sent us money for airfare to accompany them in mid-January to Maui, where they planned to celebrate their fortieth wedding anniversary. Maui certainly wasn't my holiday destination of choice, but Gord and I felt grateful enough to be able to escape the cold anywhere for ten days.

The day before we were leaving, Everett called from a phone booth.

"I could get a start on those renovations you and Gord were planning," he said. "I'd supply the labour, free, in exchange for this month's rent."

I thought of the photos Gord and I occasionally tore out of *Architectural Digest* and *Country Living* and placed in a file marked "Cabin Renovations." The photos depicted bright open kitchens with pine-and-glass cabinets and copper-sheathed counters; white-and-cream living rooms with birch bark tables and drying oregano;

gleaming studies with early 19th-century Scandinavian drop-leaf desks and black wrought-iron chandeliers.

"One of these days," Gord or I would say as we tore out these photographs, thinking of the time when we could live at the cabin year-round. The year before we had placed our income tax refunds in a special account earmarked for future renovations.

"I could get a start, at least," Everett said.

"That would probably be okay," I said. "Just wait until we get back from Maui at the end of January. Then we'll talk about what you could do."

A red light appeared on my second line. It was William Wilken, the publisher of Henday House.

"Got von Baich here," he said. "Can you come up right away?"

Paul von Baich was a University of Calgary historian who wanted us to publish a manuscript he'd written called *Western Canada: Changing Faces, Changing Places.* The manuscript explored the impact of job-related migration on traditional resource- and agriculture-based communities in Western Canada.

"Be right there," I said. Von Baich had actually produced a highly readable manuscript. I wanted to encourage William to consider it.

"I'll call you back, Everett," I said.

"No phone at the cabin, Antonia," he reminded me. "Should I call you back?"

I thought of William and Paul von Baich waiting upstairs.

"I guess you could go ahead with anything minor," I told Everett. We'd already discussed the need to replace the wainscoting and repair some cracks in the plaster.

"You betcha."

When I mentioned Everett's plans to Gord, he shook his head. "The idea of that kid roaming around the cabin with a hammer in his hand gives me the willies," he said. Gord rarely mentioned the Prociuks; he usually left me to answer any queries.

"But the labour's free," I said.

It all seems so clear now, but then I saw nothing. It was nearing the end of January, and we'd just returned from Maui where it rained more than we had expected. Gord got back to work to find that three of his customers had cancelled orders, and with the new national energy program, everyone was predicting tough times ahead in the oil patch. I was nearing the deadline for the almanac and still had some major gaps to fill on the success of recent efforts to diversify the province's economy. So neither of us had given much thought to how our tenants were faring.

The Saturday after we returned, I suggested we call the Prociuks and arrange to stop by for a few minutes. "We should just see how things are going, make sure the place isn't being trashed," I said. "We could combine it with a ski on the lake."

That afternoon we started skiing up the lake by Rundle Mission, past half a dozen relentless ice fishermen who fan out near the shore on winter weekends, driving their trucks all over the ice. All day long they sit hopefully inside cardboard Maytag boxes, over holes they cut in the ice with gasoline-powered augers, thinking about God knows what. It was one of those incandescent January days, when the snow-encrusted surface appears almost blue in the flat light.

I knocked at the cabin door, feeling awkward, like an intruder.

Dianne came to the door. She looked wan. I noticed that a pair of binoculars hung by the doorway, just as they did in our house.

"Eva's still sick," she said. "She has a fever one minute and then she has the chills. Come in."

She gestured toward the table in the kitchen. Everett was fishing on the lake, she said, hoping for some whitefish. I could see there'd been some sad little attempts at creating warmth – a jumble of family photos on the mantel, some animal prints on the wall, two Lone Star cushions on the chairs. A calendar print of A.Y. Jackson's *Frozen Lake, Early Spring, Algonquin Park* hung by the fireside in a Zeller's frame.

"One of my favorites too," I told Dianne.

Eva lay on the couch in the living room, her lank hair disappearing under an electric blanket that had seen better days. The veins on her eyelids reminded me of the delicate fissures on the lake ice. One foot, clad in a red cotton fleece sleeper, protruded from under the blanket. Dianne moved quickly to cover it.

"She loved that ornament you gave her," Dianne said. "After the tree was taken down, she said she wanted me to hang it up over her bed. So I did."

On the floor beside the couch a mass of used tissues spilled over the top of a plastic grocery bag; the bottle of generic cough syrup on the end table was the colour of congealed blood. I had hoped that the extra insulation would keep the floors warmer, but I couldn't bring myself to ask Dianne if she had noticed any difference.

Instead, I reminded myself that the former owner had stayed in the cabin over one winter. I never let myself think about his verdict: "Good thing it was mild," he'd said after we signed the papers. "It was beautiful out here, all right. Like living in a Christmas card, really. But I have to warn you, those floors never felt warm from October till May."

I recognize now that I bear guilt badly, although I hope not as badly as I used to. I think I just swallow it whole, as a child might swallow an ice cube, and that the numbing, glacial sluggishness of that guilt simply overcame my sympathy for the Prociuks.

It was different with Gord, although at the time I didn't see that either. I thought he had adopted a typically pragmatic attitude towards them, as recommended in *The Landlord's Guide to Landlord-Tenant Relations.* Only later did I realize that he thought of the Prociuks as little black dots, the dots that cluster together with other dots to form darkened masses on demographic maps, masses that trace the size and movements of migratory populations across the earth.

"Everett's been busy," Dianne said that Saturday afternoon. She motioned us down the hallway to the study. Gord didn't bother to take off his boots.

Dianne opened the door slowly, as if presenting a guest of honour. At first I couldn't see that much had changed. Two sawhorses were placed across the floor at an angle, and Everett was obviously halfway through replacing the wainscoting. A film of dust covered the floor.

And then I noticed the antique window. Everett must have found it in the trunk when he rearranged the furniture to replace the wainscoting. We'd never said anything about it; he wouldn't have known how much Gord valued it, especially since he had left it stuffed in the trunk all that time.

It looked as though Everett had tried to make the antique window fit into the frame of one of the existing windows. But the antique glass was larger than the window frame, so he had removed the lead edging and somehow managed to detach the outer band of rose-coloured hexagons, probably with glass cutters. The ravaged window looked flat, almost like plastic, without the fine lead trim and the rose hues to set it off.

"Jesus," Gord said in a low voice.

Then he started to yell: "Who the hell gave Everett permission to fool around with these windows?"

He turned around to face Dianne, then me. Neither Dianne nor I spoke. "That glasswork was early Edwardian." Gord was shouting. "A Frank Morris original, Goddammit."

His words were like lasers, freezing my flesh. Dianne didn't say anything, but her lazy left eye looked wild.

"So who gave him permission?" Gord demanded. This time he glared at Dianne.

"He told me he called," she said. "He said it was okay to go ahead with minor stuff."

Gord started to pace around the room. His ski boots sounded like jackhammers. He shoved a sawhorse out of his way; it slid and knocked over a pile of catalogues from Consumers Distributors that the Prociuks had stored in one corner. Puffs of sawdust rose up all around. I had a choking sensation in my throat.

"It was a mistake," I coughed out.

"I want you out of here by the end of the month," Gord shouted at Dianne. "And it'd be a hell of a lot sooner if I had my way."

I looked at her and, for a second, part of me wanted to put my hand on her shoulder, to reassure her that this was just another obstacle that could be weathered with time and patience, like the high interest rates and the layoffs.

But somehow I couldn't make the actions follow the feelings; my blood seemed sluggish and thickened by the strain or the cold or both. I had a vision of those beautiful rose hexagons, a helpless feeling that we would never be able to find them, or to put them back exactly as they were. And there had been no reason to destroy that beauty, that beautiful symmetry, no earthly reason at all. It was just stupidity, stupidity.

My nostrils filled with sawdust. Gord started out the door of the study. His whole body shook and his shoulders were taut. I needed some fresh air, so I just followed. It would have been the hardest thing in the world for me to have done anything else.

I heard Dianne behind me in the hallway, her footsteps hesitant. The carpet was flecked with wood shavings and clumps of snow from Gord's boots. He paused at the entrance to the living room and looked down, and the tightening in his shoulders seemed to loosen all at once. He whirled around and pounded the thin hallway wall with his fist. Three hard blows that shook the wall and knocked a calendar from a Ford dealership to the floor. Then he reached for a stacking stool just inside the living room and hurled it against the wall.

He turned to Dianne.

"Just get out," he roared, his voice thunderous. I could imagine the windows rattling, the concrete blocks beneath the floor quivering. "I want all of you out, now."

I saw her first. A flash of red cotton fleece with a parka thrown over her shoulders. She'd reached the back door by dashing through the kitchen. We were so surprised and shaken that she was nearly across the yard before any of us could move.

"You've scared her half to death, Gord," Dianne said. She pushed me against the wall to get by. At the door she almost tripped on the blanket Eva had dropped there, but steadied herself with the spring of a cat.

Both Gord and I started running too. The sight of that small figure on the ice melted the sluggishness out of me. She had no boots on, only sleepers, so her feet must have been cold by the time she reached the shore. But still she ran onto the lake ice, a small determined figure barreling toward her father somewhere in the clusters of Maytag boxes.

She was halfway to Everett's fishing hole when we saw her stumble. All I could hear was Dianne shouting at Eva and the sound of my steps pressing against the crusty ice.

One of the fishermen nearby said later he had heard the ice crack. "Just a splintering sound," he said. "Like a glass vase breaking."

One moment she was upright and running, the next moment she was gone. Her arms thrust out of the water once. Then she disappeared. Eva must have stepped onto an abandoned fishing hole.

"Help," Dianne shouted. "Someone help."

Thickly clad figures in snowmobile suits sped out of the cardboard boxes towards the spot where Eva had disappeared. I saw a form that looked like Everett's stretch flat on his belly against the ice. Another ice fishermen flung himself down on the ice and grabbed Everett's ankles.

By the time I reached the site Everett was soaked from the waist down, his head bobbing in and out of the water. Someone yelled for an ice chisel and three men ran back to retrieve more equipment.

How long Everett stayed out there, I don't know. I ran to find a telephone to call for an ambulance and the police, and to bring back warm clothing and drinks. Gord tried to organize a systematic search along grid lines but the fishermen wouldn't take the time to listen. They just started drilling all over the place.

Did she try to swim like a crazed minnow under the ice, eyes open and feet kicking? Had the burning in her lungs become unendurable? Did she hear Dianne's voice or our footsteps above the ice?

An hour and a half passed before Dianne and Everett agreed to go back to the cabin, and then only for a few minutes.

"That hole should never have been there," I heard one of the fishermen tell the Mountie. "Someone was breaking the rules, eh, drilling so close to another hole? Then you get a few days' thaw, like we did last week, and you got yourself one big hole instead of two small holes."

I was still on the ice with Dianne and Everett when the diver retrieved

Eva's body later. He discovered her in a shallow area, quite a distance from where she had fallen in.

"You don't want to see this," I said to Dianne, but she wouldn't move from where she stood, a few metres from the hole. At first the rescue team tried to block the view but Dianne said she had a right to see.

Gord and I stayed with the Prociuks most of that evening, trying to help with the arrangements. They didn't have any relatives in Alberta. It seemed the least we could do.

Only Dianne and Everett, a few of their friends from the plant and Gord and I attended the funeral. Everett didn't say much to anyone. Mostly he shook his head and repeated again and again that he couldn't believe it. He seemed too shocked to be angry, which made me feel relieved and uneasy at the same time.

Dianne's voice took on a flatness I hadn't heard before, but her gratefulness began to irritate me. "It's good of you," she said, when I took charge of organizing coffee and sandwiches in the church basement after the service. "Really, you didn't have to."

Gord hasn't said another word about the antique window, although he did ask me where I keep the safety deposit key, so I know he is checking into a possible insurance claim.

He told the Prociuks they could stay as long as they wanted, and not to worry about the rent, but they went back to Ontario right after the funeral.

So we're selling. It's the only way, with Gord on half-time and Alberta's whole economy going down the tube, thanks to Ottawa. We're prepared to sell for any price we can get.

"We'll have to box up everything we want from the study before it gets too late," I say.

But first I place the stew pot on the floor. I think I'll be able to use it again once I give it a good scrub with hot water back in the city. I retrieve a sharp knife from the kitchen, and separate the frozen mass from the container.

Surge Channels

Marguerite started across the first log of the blowdown section. Tattered bits of slippery moss clung to the bark. Someone had scored the surface long ago, but in places the marks had worn through. What must it have been like for the first Europeans who thrashed their way along this trail, she wondered? Back then, the route had only been used as a life-saving trail for survivors of shipwrecks.

She reached midpoint on the log when she heard the voices behind her. They must be close, sound didn't travel very far in the rain forest. She knew without turning who the voices belonged to. Thousands of hikers walked this remote trail on the coast of British Columbia every summer, but not many in May.

She glanced back and saw the two men from the marina. The shorter one began to cross over the same log she was on. How did they get behind her? She didn't want to think about that.

"Walk fast and you won't fall," the other man said. He had a soft, rasping chuckle.

She felt a quiver beneath her feet. Damned idiot. He was breaking the unwritten etiquette of the trail, starting to cross a narrow unsteady log while another hiker was still on it. The ski pole she had brought along instead of a walking stick wouldn't help her here, and it was a four-metre drop into the gully. She clutched for the guy wire and as she grasped it the log shook again. The other hiker must practically be jumping up and down on the same log.

She looked back again and saw the stocky man holding onto the guy wire with both hands. He gave her a broad, slow smile. Surely he hadn't deliberately shaken the log, she thought. She must be imagining things. But something about the way the man smiled made her feel unsure. Her neck felt stiff and achy.

She took even steps from log to greasy log, taking care to avoid the tangled branches and not looking at the gully below. Standing on solid ground once again, she felt the old shakiness coming over her, as it had that day on the bus a few months ago. She'd seen those other two men sitting at the back, the ones who reminded her of what had happened at Lesser Slave Lake. She'd been the only other passenger on the bus, and for a crazy moment she imagined yanking the steering wheel from the driver and steering the vehicle towards a deep ditch at the edge of the street. She'd imagined jumping out and watching as the bus rolled over with the two men aboard.

When she reached the end of the blowdown section, she looked back at the two men. One man was tall, with blunt features and a half-hearted grin; the shorter one had a thick neck and waist and straight beige hair. They were crossing the logs too quickly, their steps jerky one minute, hesitant the next. The tall one nearly fell off the last log.

"Some trail," the squat man said to Marguerite. She could see his breath in the humidity. The men had both tied running shoes outside their packs. Hers were neatly enclosed in her pack where everything was in its place, a house encased in nylon walls.

The tall hiker also carried a hatchet. She saw the handle under the cover of the pack. Perfectly natural, she thought, and felt a wave of anxiety rush through her. Christ, she thought. If I don't watch out I'll wind up like Sara.

Only this morning she had swung her backpack onto the herring boat docked at the Port Renfrew marina. She was just settling into the bow for the run across the bay when she heard the shouts. The same two men bolted out of the marina café and down the beach, heads covered in worm-green capes against the grey drizzle, each bent over with what looked to be army-issue packs. Damn. She had heard that the army sometimes used the trail for exercises.

"Jesus," the shorter man said as he scrambled onto the boat. He nearly tripped on the ski pole at the bottom, started to pitch forward, caught himself on the gunwales and winced.

"How d'ya like that?" he asked his grinning companion, offering him a Player's cigarette. "Almost an injury already. I could have sprained my goddamn thumb."

The men weren't with the army after all. The beige-haired man pushed back the hood of his cape, revealing a peaked cap that said: "Ericson's Guns and Sporting Goods" over the stitched name of a pulp mill town up the coast. He had the kind of body Marguerite would expect to see in one of the dank pubs along the Island Highway, soft and shapeless. Something about the querulous expression in the shorter man's darting eyes, and the way he smacked his lips together when he spoke, had made her bristle.

She decided to say nothing. Not her father's daughter in all ways.

They headed out across the choppy bay, a grey boat on grey water on a grey day. We're all practically invisible, Marguerite had thought. If only she could stay invisible, the world would be safe again.

Salt water sprayed on her face before they entered the calm waters of Thrasher Cove. The boat ground onto the beach. The men disembarked, the tubby one tossing a cigarette stub into the water. Then they heaved the packs onto their backs and disappeared into the rain forest. At least they wouldn't be on her heels. Small mercies.

When the fog started to lift, Marguerite saw the purplish outline of headlands across San Juan Bay and heard the low moan of the tide.

"Not a great place to be in high tide," the owner of the boat said, eyeing the tiny beach. "You got enough food for six days? Nothing out there, you know."

"I'm sure."

She'd taken his remarks as they were meant, to be helpful, even though she guessed she could have taught him a few things about survival.

The man started to help her haul the pack onto the beach but she'd insisted on handling it herself. Then she pushed the boat back into the water.

"Be careful," the man shouted. "Looks like the rain has done a pretty good job of greasing up the trail."

The beach at Thrasher Cove was deserted. Driftwood logs as thick as barrels were piled against the flank of high brown cliffs. She turned back to look at the water, imagining the rhythm of the waves soothing her spine.

In one way, at least, she was her father's daughter. A person needed some time for idling, for the inner renewal of natural beauty, he said. She was twelve the first time he took her on the Skyline Trail in Jasper.

When they reached Shovel Pass, he swung his arm to encompass an arc of ink-blue mountain peaks. "Petrarch, Francis of Assisi – they knew the strength you could draw from nature," he said. Ever the history professor.

When she had taken off her boots that first night in the tent, her father saw a blister on her left heel and scolded her for not telling him about it. She'd said she was sorry. But she'd never admitted the real reason why she hadn't mentioned the blister, even though the pain was excruciating. She was afraid that if she complained, he wouldn't take her up there again.

Right away Marguerite had known she would seek out places like this all her life. She even had days when she thought that, at thirty-two, she had managed to shape the life she wanted. She worked as a limnologist for the Alberta government, taking water samples from remote lakes and streams. Sometimes she had to drive all-terrain vehicles on bumpy gravel roads to reach the bodies of water that needed sampling. In winter she was issued a snowmobile. Every couple of weeks she went back to the lab in Edmonton to analyse and document the data.

That's how it used to be, anyway. Before Slave Lake.

For three hours she had fought her way from Thrasher Cove to the blowdown section. All along the way the trail oozed with mud, rotting undergrowth and occasional droppings from small animals. Giant hemlock, spruce and cedar so filtered the light that she felt she was viewing the world through green-tinted lenses. If Sara could have been there for one minute, she recalled thinking. It would have been worth it, just to have seen the expression on her face.

Sleeves of mist hung beneath the tree tops. Here and there patches of salal burst into green sprays, waist high. Branches strewn with moss brushed her shoulders. Marguerite's T-shirt clung to her back, sticky from the humidity and the exertion. Vapour covered the lenses of her Leica binoculars.

Every few steps, gnarled, ankle-clutching roots thrust out of the muck, the trickster hands of subterranean demons. She almost tripped over a root but steadied herself with the yellow ski pole Sara insisted she bring it along, instead of her father's antique brass-tipped hickory walking stick. "That way you can use it as a spear in case you run out of food," Sara had laughed as they cleaned out instruments at the lab last week. Sara's brother had done the trail once, so naturally she considered herself an expert. Marguerite had to admit that she liked the way the fibreglass pole felt, cool and smooth and solid against her palm, a kind of anchor. The two men who took the boat over to the trailhead with her hadn't bothered to carry walking sticks, she'd noticed, even though hikers broke hips on this trail, sprained ankles, smashed knees. A few even died, drowned in the sucking current of Nitinat Narrows, slipping off thin log bridges into deep chasms, caught on ledges, trapped against the cliffs by rising tides or flung from rocks by rogue waves.

She patted her front pocket, bulky with the tide tables and topographical maps of this rugged stretch of Pacific coast. For a moment she'd seen herself as a fugitive in some long-ago dark green underground tunnel to freedom, although some people – people like Sara – would call freedom a funny name for what she was in for. She could care less what they thought; she hoped only that somewhere ahead, last year would disappear, along with the compulsive over-the-shoulder glances, the stiffness she carried in her neck since Slave Lake. They didn't call it the lifesaving trail for nothing.

It was already four o'clock by the time she reached the great masses of trunks, twisted and criss-crossed, which the guidebook described as the blowdown section. Blowdown sections were caused by logging companies allowed to log within a kilometre of the shoreline, the book explained. Trees protect themselves from blowdowns by something called "wind pruning" – growing so evenly that the forceful ocean winds passed overhead instead of swirling furiously into open spaces.

Marguerite recalled a rush of pleasure as she stared at the blowdown area. Since leaving the trailhead her veins felt cleaner, as if sweat and humidity and exertion had pumped her blood hard enough, fast enough, to clear away that toxic memory from last year.

And then those two men from the marina appeared behind her. They'd probably stopped at one of the viewpoints and she'd passed them without knowing it. All completely innocent.

"Of course it is," she could hear Sara's voice saying inside her head, her voice supple with mockery. "They're just as innocent as seal pups."

Sara also worked at the lab as a technologist, although she didn't do any field work. Like Marguerite, she was divorced and lived alone. Unlike Marguerite, she liked staying in the lab, knowing where she would be each day and what she would be doing.

"The lab is like being back in the womb," Sara joked.

One time, when Marguerite was having her house painted, she stayed over at Sara's for a couple of nights. Sara insisted that she sleep in her room while she took the couch. When Marguerite made up the bed, she was startled to find a steel letter opener under the pillow. It looked as lethal as a dagger.

Then, at Christmas, Sara had given her a metal letter opener from a nature club catalogue, topped with a jaunty copper-wrought fox. Marguerite put the letter opener where she opens letters, in a pencil container on her kitchen counter.

She sat down on a damp fallen log at the end of the blowdown section and waited for ten minutes to give the two men time to get well ahead of her. Beyond the blowdown area, the forest soon became thin and stunted, and she could hear the faint sound of waves. She decided not to try to make it to the campground. She'd rather establish her own camp, somewhere private where she could watch for seals and explore the tidal shelf life and not worry about anybody watching.

Coming out onto the open, she saw a line of basalt cliffs above the narrow sandstone shelf that separated the forest from the ocean. If she backtracked a bit, she should be able to climb to the cliff tops and set up there, at the lip of the forest. No point thinking of camping on the flat rock-shelf. It could be dangerous at high tide.

She found an excellent campsite in a sheltered clearing high above the rain-slicked rocks. In the distance the washed lavender tongue of the peninsula jutted out to the ocean. The air was pine-scented. For a moment Marguerite thought she saw seals out on the lead-grey water, but realized they were only bulbous floating heads of kelp. Two northern ravens swooped above.

It started to rain lightly. She erected the tent, used her jack knife to cut four lengths of cord and tied a plastic tarp between two spruce trees to create a dry cooking area. Then she lit the gasoline stove and cooked freeze-dried couscous and chicken.

The rain stopped after dinner. She burned the paper wrappers from the meal, then took coffee in a plastic mug down to the rocks. A cool wind blew and the moon was an ice-hued wedge. The tide was coming in. Grey waves pummelled the rock shelf. She was thankful she didn't have to camp down there, as survivors of shipwrecks had a century ago.

Somewhere not too far up the coast, on a night like this, in thick weather with heavy seas and a high tide running, almost ninety years ago, the Valencia foundered. Bound from San Francisco to Victoria, an iron steamship with 108 passengers and a crew of 65. Most of the lifeboats were lost in the night. Some people huddled on the ship while the few who got to shore struggled to stay warm or raced down this trail to summon help from Victoria. But by the time help came, all the people left on the ship had been flung into the sea. A loss of 136 people, no women and children surviving.

A light drizzle began again and she retreated into the tent. It had been more than a year now since she had camped out by herself. She stretched her toes against the bottom of the sleeping bag and felt a delicious coolness. The old ecstasy returning.

She'd get up early tomorrow, so she'd have some time to investigate the tide pools: watery kaleidoscopes of sea urchins, coralline algae, ochre starfish, blue-shelled mussels, green anemones, bright yellow sea lemons. But lying in the tent, she felt oddly wakeful. She heard the rush of the tide at the bottom of the cliff, and wind brushing the thick-matted ceiling of the forest. Sometimes she heard tree trunks rubbing together, like the wails of the Druids mourning. Sometimes she heard the patter of small animals skittering around the edges of the tent. She dreamed of sea-green hatchets, swooping ravens and sea lions perched on top of lighthouses, bellowing deep-throated storm warnings.

She woke early. The sun was white and hazy, casting a silvery sheen on an ocean as smooth as a sheet pulled tight. She walked to the edge of the cliff. At first she couldn't make out the round mushroomlike formation on the rock shelf. And then, through the binoculars, she identified two khaki packs leaning against a pile of driftwood. The Fort Renfrew pair. They had spent the night only one hundred metres away.

A free world, she thought. At least they hadn't disturbed her, played radios like some jerks she's known.

It was only later, when she started to strike the tent, that she noticed a cigarette butt a few steps away. She picked it up, like all the garbage she found on the trail, planning to burn it later. It was the stub from a Player's cigarette, and it looked recent. But it didn't really mean anything, Marguerite thought. Some other hiker might have left it Or the two might have hiked in this way before she arrived. She tried not to think about what an out-of-the-way place this was, about how she had chosen this spot precisely because she thought it unlikely that other hikers would come anywhere near.

Then she felt something soft under her foot. She'd stepped on a green slug, one of the notorious West Coast variety. Gooey pus appeared to be running from its mashed head. Marguerite wiped the sole against the grass. Her head spun. She wouldn't do any idling here this morning.

She'd try to find a place of her own later today.

What she wanted now, more than anything, was to put some time between herself and the Port Renfrew pair.

Two years ago, she had actually been featured in a career brochure, designed to encourage students to consider a wide range of environmental careers.

"What do you like most about your job?" the interviewer asked, trying to get her to say something that would stroke his democratic, do-gooder agenda, maybe about contributing to the environment or to society as a whole. "The outdoors," she'd said. "The opportunity to be on my own, outdoors, away from all the riffraff."

If only she could take the wider view. But if anything she feels narrower in the wilderness, more protective of her turf, even less tolerant. One time, she and her father came across a teen-aged boy on a mountain trail. The boy had a dirty face and carried a big hunting knife, and he was scraping away a big circle of bark. The creamy wood beneath the bark looked like butter-soft calfskin.

"You're hurting the tree," she had cried. But her father motioned for her to keep quiet, and they walked on.

"But he was hurting the tree," she said.

Her father had stopped and looked at her. "Yes, he was hurting the tree," he said. "But not a great deal."

And then he'd said that the boy might learn so much about the tree through his afternoon activities that he wouldn't want to hurt it anymore.

"Whereas if we order him around, he might just turn against us – and all this." And he'd motioned to the mountains and the river valley below.

She nodded. She imagined herself with the knife in her hand, defending the tree. She wished she could be like her father, able to take the wider view.

The rain forest was dark and cool, alive with bird song, dripping with dew. Sunlight filtered in from the green filigree, casting patches of light on her bare arms and legs. She looked over her shoulder often, hated herself for doing so.

She reached Camper Bay just before lunch. From the trail, she could see small figures on the beach below, other campers taking a morning off, drying their Lycra underwear, enjoying the first sunshine for a week. This morning she was actually thankful for the sight of other people.

To get down to the beach, she first had to walk across a swinging suspension bridge, then manoeuvre down two ladders. Two hundred rungs in all, she'd read. The rungs were greasy, and the pack's shoulder straps cut into her flesh. The second day out on the trail was always hard. She learned that from her father. She threw the ski pole down to the ground and it made a soft thud.

A creek ran into the ocean, and Marguerite saw a few tents beside it. She walked on to a sunny part of the beach, near a small tidal pool, and took off her boots and socks. When she dipped her feet into the pool, they tingled from the cold. She dried her feet carefully, then stretched out against a log and ate her lunch.

The bay was bounded by a sharp peninsula which Marguerite knew led to a narrow rock shelf. Depending on the time of day you reach this point, the guidebook said, you could either hike on the coastal shelf, known for its glorious pink-tiled tidal pools and its deep chasms which can be difficult to cross, or you could take the forest path, which was dark and dull, but which would make her more invisible, more protected. Then she could camp at the designated campground.

She thought of the cigarette filter outside the tent. She'd take the forest route. It wasn't what she'd planned, that day she'd seen the letter opener under Sara's pillow and decided she never wanted to live that way. But it was the sensible way.

A bare-chested older man in nylon jogging shorts is dragging a log along the beach. He has grey hair and wire spectacles. Except for part of a neatly coiled rope, no odd bits of equipment protrude from his pack.

"Gorgeous day," he says.

"Gorgeous," Marguerite agrees.

"You taking the forest or the beach?" asks the man, who introduces himself as Tim. His voice reminds her of lecture halls and campus wine and cheese parties.

"The forest," she replies. "Because of all the chasms."

"My son and I are making a bridge," Tim says. "Should be able to clear the first surge channel in about twenty minutes, if we're lucky. Then we'll make another bridge over the chasm at the other end. You can come along, if you want."

She feels the sun's warmth on her cheek. How good it feels to be out of the forest. If she takes the rock-shelf route, she might be able to identify the point where the Puritan went down in 1896. She knows the story by heart, how the four-masted schooner became stranded on Bonilla Point, how a lone Indian appeared and managed to grapple a line from the stern of the ship and so rig a lifeline to shore.

She notices that the rock at the point, where sea lions sunned when she first came down to the beach, is no longer visible. Tim seems to read her mind.

"Tide's coming in. We'd better get a move on. You coming?"

She is about to say no when she observes two hikers coming down the ladder. The pair from Port Renfrew.

The walking will be a lot faster on the shelf, she reasons. If she goes that route, instead of through the forest, she'll gain a good two hours on that pair. It's unlikely they would follow along the rock shelf. The guidebook warns against choosing that route this time of day. The surge channels, deep cuts in the rock shelf, can be difficult to cross, the book says. If you don't pay close attention to the tide tables, you could be trapped against the cliff by the incoming tide. The cliffs along the shelf are too steep and slippery to climb.

"Yes, thanks," she says, hoisting on her pack. She follows Tim and his teen-aged son, Paul, along the sandstone shelf to the site of the first surge channel. Tide water roars and swirls into the chasm, which is about two metres wide and two metres deep and extends across the shelf to the base of the cliffs. Tim and Paul heave two thigh-thick logs across the narrowest section. The second log misses the far edge and clatters down into the channel. It bobs in the churning waves and clunks against the rocks.

Tim straddles the remaining log and shimmies across. She recognizes in him the steadiness she often observed in her father. Paul crosses with his father's ease and Marguerite follows. The log is wet and rough against her thighs.

"Should we burn our bridges?" she asks, pointing to the log.

Tim looks surprised.

"Better leave them," he replies. "Who knows, someone else may be coming. Besides, the tide will soon wash it away. It's only about forty minutes till high tide."

They walk on the shelf wordlessly for twenty minutes or so. Tongues of tidewater press in. They'd better be able to cross the next surge channel, she thinks, because soon the tide will be so high they won't be able to return the way they came. She looks up at the steep cliffs and is thankful she and Tim have paid such close attention to the tide tables. If they weren't attuned to the rhythm of the ocean, they could so easily have found themselves trapped between the tide and the smooth rock.

The second surge channel is no wider than the first but deeper, at least three metres, and smooth-walled as ice. She helps Tim and Paul push driftwood logs across the chasm. At first they can hardly budge the logs, which are bigger than the ones they moved before. Tim places some small logs under the large ones to act as rollers.

Tim crosses, then the boy. It's her turn. She feels a spit of ocean spray on her ankles, and then she's across. The shelf gives way to a wide, safe pebble beach backed by driftwood that extends above the high tide line. They should be able to hike safely along here for the rest of the day, Tim says. Probably they will have it all to themselves.

"See you," he says. Tim and Paul are soon around the next point and out of sight.

Marguerite takes off her pack to rest for a moment, and notices two figures behind her in the distance. She reaches for her binoculars. The Port Renfrew pair again. They probably didn't even bother to bring tide tables.

In the pounding of the ocean she hears her blood pumping, sees the Player's cigarette butt again by the tent. And then she's walking along the trail by Slave Lake, her water samples in her pack, thinking that it's fifteen minutes back to the jeep and another thirty minutes till she can get a shower. That's when she passes the two men on the trail. They must have slipped up from the lake. They each carry rainbow trout, a mass of gleaming scales. She is about a dozen strides ahead of them when it strikes her that the men are carrying more than their limit.

"Excuse me," she calls back. "Aren't you over your limit?"

The men shrug. To hell with them, she thinks. She'd report them on her cellular as soon as she got back to the jeep.

She continues along the trail which is shaded by swaying black poplar and banked by a thicket of red-osier dogwood. The breeze from across the lake has a refreshing bite. And then, in a moment that seems like five, a hand clamps over her mouth and an arm reaches around her waist. Her nostrils fill with a fishy odor tinged with sweat and aftershave.

"Don't say a word." The rasp of a man's voice. The back of her head pressed against hard metal buttons, a rough denim sleeve against her jaw.

Another voice, softer. There are two of them. "We need to teach this cunt a lesson," says the man with the softer voice.

She knows how it will be, how she'll be dragged into the brush, how one man will gag her and pin her arms as the other strips off her jeans and rips away her underwear. She knows they sometimes take turns. She imagines the clutch of stubby, fishy fingers on her crotch, the heaving sour breath, the press of bodies, and all the time the snickers and the tearing. She can barely breathe.

They start to drag her towards the brush. But for a moment one man lifts his hand off her mouth and she screams so loudly she can hardly believe the force of her lungs, and she's aware of some other sound cutting in, perhaps the gunning of an engine or someone starting a generator down the lake, she's not sure. At the instant the two sounds fuse the two men stare at each other and that's all the opportunity she needs.

Later, at the police station, she filed her report. The police officer told her to take all the time she needed, but she wondered why she was bothering at all.

"I just wish I'd had my knife in my hand," she'd told him.

"Oh no," the police officer said. He held up his hand as if she were a child thinking of walking against a red light. "It's better that you didn't."

He thought she was lucky, he said. To have escaped.

But of course she hadn't. When she went home to her apartment, she noticed for the first time the size of the shadows cast by the Manitoba maples along the street where she lived. She started taking her Honda to the lab instead of walking. She told herself it would just be for a few weeks, till she got over the shock. But she was still driving. Of course the men had never been apprehended.

Marguerite found she didn't want to do field work up at Slave Lake or anywhere else for a while. "Let me stay in the lab," she'd told Joan, her supervisor, citing paperwork that needed to be done. Joan had agreed.

And then she'd started delaying the date that she would return to the field. First she had the flu. Then she was in the middle of a big research project and didn't want to leave. Eight months have passed. If she doesn't get back soon, Joan says she'll have to advertise for someone else to fill the position.

The sea is dazzling. She is a little dizzy, has a sense of drifting, like a ship without anchor or one of those bulbous heads of kelp. She thinks she might not have enough strength to move the log over the chasm, but she spies a smaller log to use as a roller. The sun glints off the tidal pools and she shields her eyes. She pries the big log up with the aid of the ski pole, slips the smaller log beneath it and pushes it with all her strength.

The log splashes deep into the chasm and churning blue-green sea water surges in, foam flecked, angry and swirling. Human cries will be nothing against the crash of the incoming tide. She walks on. The metal point of the ski pole clicks against the sea-rounded pebbles, and she remembers what Sara said about it acting as a spear.

Gail Helgason

Gail Helgason is a Saskatchewan native now living in Edmonton, where she works as a journalist. A graduate of the University of Saskatchewan and Carleton University's journalism school, she has written a history, *The First Albertans*, and co-authored three travel books with her husband, writer/editor John Dodd.

Helgason's short stories have appeared in a number of literary magazines, but this is her first book of fiction. Like the characters in her stories, she's an avid hiker, cyclist, canoeist, and cross-country skier.

About the Cover Artist

Dan Hudson graduated from York University with a Bachelor of Fine Arts degree in 1983. His paintings have been featured in numerous solo and groups exhibition across Canada, including *Call of the Wild* at the Walter Phillips Gallery in Banff. Hudson lives in Canmore, Alberta.